Faith HEALER

Other titles by Victoria G. Smith

Warrior Heart, Pilgrim Soul:
An Immigrant's Journey (poetry)

The Driftless Unsolicited Novella Series

Technologies of the Self   Haris A. Durrani

Faith Healer   Victoria G. Smith

Faith Healer

VICTORIA G. SMITH

The Driftless Unsolicited Novella Series
BRAIN MILL PRESS · GREEN BAY, WISCONSIN

Published in the United States by Brain Mill Press.
ISBN 978-1-942083-30-6
EPUB ISBN 978-1-942083-32-0
MOBI ISBN 978-1-942083-31-3
PDF ISBN 978-1-942083-33-7

Cover illustration © Hannah Irlbeck.
Cover design by Ranita Haanen.
Interior design by Williams Writing, Editing & Design.

www.brainmillpress.com

The Driftless Unsolicited Novella Series of Brain Mill Press publishes those novellas selected as winners of the Driftless Unsolicited Novella Contest each year.

To my childhood friend, Father John Bovenmars, MSC,
who humored a precocious, curious young girl
and taught her about angels.

CONTENTS

Faith HEALEr

PROLOGUE

"Open up, Victor! You bastard homo freak! You negro psychic quack!" The angry mob outside screamed, banging and rattling on the gate of his townhouse. Victor was glad that in addition to the solid metal gate, a tall concrete fence banded at the top by barbed wire and broken glass protected his residence. The people had begun to turn against those who collaborated with the corrupt Marcos regime. And wouldn't he be considered one of the more notorious—being the alleged Rasputin of the dictatorship? "No Madam or Sir to protect you now, huh? They're going down, and so are you!" The mob sounded like it was getting bigger and more agitated. Elsewhere in the city, similar vengeful crowds were storming and looting Malacañang Palace, grabbing whatever they could from what had been left behind by the dictator and his family, whom they believed had been stealing from them for more than two decades.

Victor had only enough time to throw a few clothes and other necessities into a carry-on suitcase, making sure he didn't forget his Philippine passport stamped with a U.S. visa, a thousand dollars in cash, a plane ticket to Los Angeles, and—despite feeling orphaned, this time, by God himself—the statue of El Negro Santo Niño de Jesus, the Black Child Jesus. He wrapped the *santo* in several layers of clothing to cushion it. After some internal tug-of-war, he slipped the ancient medallion strung on a gold chain around his neck and stowed away the pair of sacred stones from Mount Banahaw into a side pocket of his luggage—mere souvenirs now of the dream life he'd had. In another pocket, he shoved the black-and-white photo that held the curse and riddle of his life. But he passed on the tarot cards and other tools of his trade. He wouldn't need them anymore. Not ever. They were, after all, mere props for his deceit.

The visa, plane ticket, and money were parting gifts from the Madam in gratitude for his long and loyal service. No, she couldn't take him in the same plane that would carry her and her family to Hawaii, courtesy of the U.S. government. "But here, take these at least," she'd said, hugging and kissing him on both cheeks, leaving on his skin and clothes the residue of her favorite scent, Chanel No. 5. "And pray, pray to the Santo Niño that Ferdie and I will return to save all of you from these *ingratos,* these thankless savages." She had carefully dabbed the corners of her eyes with a Kleenex to prevent her makeup from running. Even in defeat, she was elegantly dressed, brilliantly bejeweled, and perfectly made up. Her signature teased and brushed-up coiffure proudly displayed her high cheekbones, Spanish eyes, and the porcelain complexion that had earned her the Miss Manila title in her youth and won her the heart of the then-young senator from Ilocos who would practically become the Filipino king.

If there was anything that broke her heart nearly as much as her husband's ouster, it might have been that she had to leave a thousand pairs of Italian shoes in her Malacañang closet. Once, Victor recalled her musing in an unguarded moment, "When I was a little girl, I only had one pair of shoes, and I had to wear them till there were holes in them and my feet hurt. I don't want my feet to hurt anymore, Victor." He'd nodded in sympathy with her, for he knew firsthand what it meant to be poor. Her extravagant lifestyle in the midst of her people's poverty, however, had earned her the reputation of an Eva Perón. That was why, Victor now understood, the movie *Evita* was banned from Philippine movie houses all those years.

Without the bodyguards who used to protect him from the crowds—once adoring, now turned hateful—Victor gave thanks for the evening shadows that camouflaged him as he squeezed out of a rear second-floor window to climb down a sturdy old bougainvillea. He stifled his cries as the thorns of the woody vine pierced his fingers, tore his clothes, scraped his skin. *Damn that I've been reduced to this,* he thought. *Leaving my own home like a thief in the night!* All the expensive furniture, antiques, and imported accessories inside his house would now go to the dogs. But better them than him!

Victor jumped down onto a little-known access path that led to the back side of the block where he lived. Limping initially, he retrieved the luggage he had earlier lowered by rope and walked away at a measured pace, careful not to call attention to himself. He'd studied and planned this route well. The bulk of the protesting crowds were permanently camped on EDSA Boulevard, where CNN cameras tirelessly filmed the Philippine People's Power Revolution in progress. As for the mob in front of his house, he figured there was no easy way for it to detect his escape and get to him without breaking down the gate or jumping the fence.

The "revolution," as Victor had come to understand it from the news, was primarily a civil disobedience movement aimed at pressuring President Ferdinand Marcos and his cronies to give up the reins of government and pave the way for democratic elections. People boycotted work and school and held candlelight vigils in the streets, broadcasting rosary prayers from loudspeakers—the Filipino version of Gandhi's nonviolent revolution. Street barbeques, beer drinking, disco music, and karaoke—not to mention flower offerings to smiling soldiers manning army tanks—made for a fiesta atmosphere unlike any revolution the world had ever seen. And lest anyone mistake this as other than a wholesome family affair, parents handed over their children to the soldiers to sit with them on the tanks, their happy little feet dangling from cannon snouts.

Only Filipinos could turn a potentially dangerous situation into an excuse for a party, Victor had thought as he sat, a helpless prisoner in his own home until he'd mustered the courage to request the Madam's help in exiting the country. Even he was amazed when the so-called revolution succeeded in forcing the cunning, long-entrenched dictator and his family into exile with hardly a shot fired or blood spilled. Everyone called it a miracle. The capricious gods had switched loyalties at last—the same gods he used to call upon in service to his ousted masters. *The same ones who favored me in youth and abandoned me when I needed them most.*

He moved through the dark, potholed, urine-soaked Mabini streets, mindful that someone could still be watching and following him. He had dressed to avoid recognition. While his regular wardrobe consisted of designer trousers and a black crewneck shirt under a light-colored linen blazer, his face masked and adorned by black Wayfarer shades day and night, fancying he looked like a mere darker version of *Miami Vice*'s Don Johnson, he now wore generic denims, a simple cotton T-shirt under an all-weather black jacket, and an old baseball hat to hide his face.

He spied four men drinking beer at a corner *sari-sari* store. His heart beat so loud in his ears, Victor failed to catch what one of the men hollered out at him. Ignoring them, Victor crossed the street and continued as nonchalantly as he could. The man, sounding utterly drunk, yelled louder, "*Hoy, bakla,* where are you going? I was talking to you! I said, which darling are you going to see at this time of the night? Why—no more pretty boys around here for you?" His buddies guffawed. The man stumbled toward Victor, tripping a few times before finally blocking Victor's path.

It always disturbed him—that derisive label, *bakla.* Apparently his effeminate gait had given him away as a homosexual, though he didn't consider himself one. But the word could save him now. It meant the men didn't recognize him. So he played along, languidly sweeping up a hand in the characteristic manner of openly feminine gay men, flirtatiously replying, "Oh, c'mon, *Manong.* To me, you are all *guwapo.* All handsome, indeed! Sadly, I'm going to visit my sick mother, so please let me be on my way."

"Not until you pay the toll," the drunk said in a naughty, singsong voice. He chuckled and wagged a forefinger close to Victor's face.

"What toll?" Victor backstepped in panic as the two other men likewise surrounded him.

"This toll." The drunk unzipped his pants, acting as if he was about to take a miserably flaccid, stinky thing out of the flaps.

Just in time, a thundering roar and intense glare of a headlight disoriented Victor's bullies. He swung his suitcase straight into the groin of the drunk before him, sending the man to the ground crying and cursing and knocking down at least one of his buddies. The tricycle—that ubiquitous, agile vehicle of the poor consisting of a motorcycle with a sidecar—that Victor had ordered masterfully scooped up its passenger and zoomed away before the men could stop them. He sighed in relief as he settled into the tricycle's passenger seat. It wasn't the Mercedes Benz limousine he was used to traveling about in under the Madam's auspices, but it did the job. The two hundred pesos he'd promised his young driver was well worth it. *"Maraming salamat,"* he said in thanks. "That was a good getaway."

The boy beamed. *"Ayos lang,* boss! No problem."

When they reached the airport, Victor handed him an extra fifty-peso tip.

CHAPTER 1

"Tita Vee! Tita Vee!" the old woman in room 105 cheerfully cries out as he passes by with his cleaning cart. Victor retraces his steps and peeks into the open door, where he finds her sitting in her rocking chair, knitting. The rocker beats rhythmically with the clicking of her needles.

"Tita Vee" is the nickname he took on when he arrived at this place—*Tita* being the Filipino term of endearment for an aunt. At first, he'd meant it to be used by his younger fellow employees as a way of establishing a more personal connection with them, but the name soon stuck with everyone.

"Why, Mrs. Langley! You're looking super today, my dear. You seem unusually bright. What's your secret?"

She giggles and shoos away his words in a motion of affected modesty. But Victor knows he's succeeded in flattering the old lady. He likes to caress the old folks with sweet words. This is how he became popular at the Casa del Sol Retirement Villas in Thousand Oaks, California, where he's employed as both a janitor and caregiver, a position custom-made for him. Many of the elderly residents hardly get enough attention from their own families, and he knows he's well disposed to give it. It's an easy thing for him to do, costs him nothing, and best of all, makes people happy. He also believes this makes him indispensable—which is a good thing, for he badly needs to keep this job. Some might call it pandering, but he doesn't think himself dishonest when he does it, for God knows he tries not to give empty praise as much as he can help it. He learned long ago—when he realized his fate and fortune depended on what came out of his mouth—that when one looks closely enough at even the ugliest and most charmless creatures, one can see some good in them, or at least what passes for good. He certainly has a lot of training in this regard in respect to his former masters' cronies, their wives, and their mistresses, many of whom had absolutely nothing to their merit except their cunning and wealth—most of it ill-gotten under the dictator's tutelage.

"Did you know it's my great-granddaughter's birthday in a couple of weeks?" Mrs. Langley asks, snatching Victor back to the present. "You remember Chrissie, my little cutie pie, who visited me the other Sunday?"

"Yes, yes, of course," Victor replies, reminded of the tsunami disaster masquerading as a six-year-old girl. The melted chocolate ice cream all over Mrs. Langley's room, the pink chewing gum stuck on the carpet and linoleum floors that took forever to scrape off, the broken vase in the lobby, the complaints from the other residents about the girl who'd entered their rooms and vandalized their things—how could anyone forget her? Especially the one who had to clean up after her.

"Oh, I'm so excited, an idea just came to me!" exclaims Mrs. Langley. "Since I won't be able to attend Chrissie's birthday party at that fun center with her little friends, you know what would be a perfect way for me to celebrate her birthday? Can you guess what I'm thinking? Can you?" The old lady claps, as if to urge Victor to hurry on reading her mind.

"Hmm. Oh, I give up! Just tell me, honey—for only God can keep up with that delightful, pretty little head of yours." He tenderly cups one side of Mrs. Langley's hairdo, admiring the new cut and perm on her short, natural platinum hair. Catching a glimpse of his own reflection in a mirror, he grimaces at the sight of salt-and-pepper streaks in the fried ball of hair on his head. *Alas, that's what pushing forty looks like.* He badly needs a trim and a dye job, but he can't seem to find the time for the first, and he's loath to spend his meager salary on the second. He reminds himself to buy some hair dye at the drugstore on his next time off. If he's learned to reinvent himself into a caregiver and part-time janitor, he can certainly learn to dye his own hair.

Mrs. Langley giggles. "Why, I'll have a party for her *here.* Here! Isn't that a wonderful idea, Tita Vee?"

Victor wants to say, *Oh, boy, that'll be something—having that hurricane Chrissie get a sugar load at a party here.* Instead, he says, "Yes, of course! Why, you don't just have a pretty little head—you're also one smart cookie!" He plants his hands on his hips and with mock sternness asks, "Now, speaking of smart—have you taken your pills yet, young lady?"

"Yes, silly billy! I don't intend to drop dead just before my Chrissie's birthday."

"That's a good plan," Victor says, chuckling.

"Will you help me to put the party together?"

"You didn't even need to ask, sweetie. Now get yourself a good nap before they ring for dinner." He puts away her knitting in the basket next to her chair, helps her into bed, and covers her white, bony knees with a throw.

Later, after stowing away his cleaning cart, Victor retreats into the quiet semidarkness of his bedroom on the rear side of the main building. His day duties are over, and he has a couple of hours' rest before his next assignment. This is one reason he can't afford to lose this job—the rare benefit of having on-site private quarters. Rent in California is no joke, as he'd discovered on arrival. He'd hesitated to accept the Casa del Sol position after he learned exactly how much his salary was going to be, expressing worry to his then-prospective employers that he'd be able to find an affordable place to live in the affluent area. He was lucky that the Indian couple who owned the retirement home were the ones who interviewed him for the janitorial position. They must have either immediately liked him or readily recognized a good yet desperate person they could exploit, for they offered him, right there and then, the privilege of room and board in return for twenty-four-hour on-call duty and Victor's willingness to do almost anything and everything that needed to be done. Victor couldn't believe his good luck and so immediately agreed. He realized when he got his first paycheck that the monetary value of his room and board was deducted from his monthly pay, which left him with almost no spending cash. Still, the arrangement is a creative solution to his housing problem. A roof over his head and food for his belly are his priorities, anyway, and clothing needs are a nonissue since Casa del Sol provides for and requires its staff to wear uniforms. Victor is content with his perpetual beige overalls—a far cry from his Don Johnson outfit many years ago, but sufficient.

The biggest disadvantage to all these privileges, of course, is lack of privacy and time off. Everyone seems to feel free to knock on his door at all times of the day and night, for one thing or another. Office clerks, activities directors, and sometimes even medication dispensers and physical therapists appear to have no scruples about calling in sick or taking last-minute leaves, knowing Tita Vee will always be there to cover for them. He consoles himself with the thought that he has the opportunity to learn various aspects of the caregiving business, which he imagines will serve him well if he has to one day abruptly leave this job to go elsewhere—a constant worry in his mind. He's sure his capricious yet mandatory work schedule violates some California labor laws, but beggars can't be choosers, he reminds himself, especially not TNTs, or *tago-nang-tagos,* like him—those who are always hiding, the Filipinos' label for illegal immigrants.

He takes off his gray plastic-rimmed eyeglasses and presses the inside corners of his eyes. It's that headache again. He lies on his cot, and soon enough, his mind wanders off into the past, as it usually does.

Oh, Peachy, why'd you have to leave me, too?

CHAPTER 2

When he'd arrived at LAX five years earlier, Victor had nowhere to go, no one to turn to. He stayed two days at the terminal just phoning and waiting to hear from Filipino acquaintances he knew resided in the Los Angeles area, but when he said it was Victor Mariano calling, they either hung up or offered excuses—they weren't in very good circumstances either, or they didn't have enough room in their homes to accommodate him. "Don't you know anyone else?" they said, more like a demand than a question.

Sure, he knew a lot of old friends of the Madam who'd come to him for prognostications and other consultations at a time when his name was famously linked to that of the First Family. But all those so-called old friends shunned him now, just as they shunned the Madam in the end. *Oh, Victor, it's nothing personal. We're all in the same boat, you see. We're starting from scratch, too. We left behind much of what we owned in the Philippines, our money frozen by the new government. Do you know how risky it is these days for small people like us to take in someone as big and important as you? We have children and jobs to think of, you understand,* and so on and so forth. The hypocrites! There was a time when they'd line up for days to get a card or palm reading from him or have an ailment cured, ready to pay his "donation" fee of five hundred pesos an hour. *Small people indeed.* They'd strutted themselves in their gold, diamonds, and pearls, claiming favors from the Madam or Sir and then asking Victor to please assure them fate continued to smile on them. Now they didn't even have the decency to offer him a bed or a couch for the night or a warm meal to welcome him. It was incredible to him that his ostracism had reached as far as the United States.

On his third day at the airport, a flicker of hope sparked through the miserable pay-phone line. Someone mentioned the name of a long-lost friend Victor knew had settled in Los Angeles some years back: Peachy Gonzales. Fortunately, this someone had saved an address where Victor's friend might be found.

Peachy was once a famous Filipino couturier—Victor would argue, the greatest the Philippines ever had—who'd built a fortune as one of Madam's exclusive designers by the time Victor had entered the Marcos dynasty scene. He came to understand that Peachy's wealth and fame were the products not so much of his creative talent, extraordinary good luck, or entrepreneurial genius, all of which, while instrumental to Peachy's discovery by the Madam—who'd taken him out of his rabbit hole of a dress shop in Binondo and installed him in a plush Makati couturier's den that Peachy swiftly turned into a fashion conglomerate—were, rather, the outcome of his uncanny clarity of vision.

Since Victor and Peachy frequently found themselves in each other's company as part of Madam's entourage, their acquaintance had many opportunities to grow into the deep friendship it became. First, they were useful to each other. Victor treated Peachy's gallstones and the severe arthritis caused by all the fine embroidery work Madam's clothes required. In turn, Peachy helped Victor transition and fit into Madam's social circle by serving as a guide to the different personalities that surrounded their patron. "Do not for one second believe they think of us as their equals," Peachy admonished of the members of Madam's social circle. "For to them, we are merely the freak side circus that exists purely for Madam's pleasure. When we don't serve that purpose anymore or the Marcoses lose their power—which they will—you can be sure we'll be nothing again to them." How true this all proved for Victor.

Five years older than Victor, Peachy assumed the role of elder brother to him—or, perhaps more properly, elder sister, as Peachy was a homosexual who sometimes liked to dress in women's clothes. The lighthearted camaraderie they shared evolved into an unspoken recognition that they were not merely serendipitous friends but sibling misfit souls. They fancied themselves belonging perhaps to some mystic clan of lost heroes, only temporarily kept from their true calling, but surely inching toward a glorious destiny together. Thus, when Peachy announced he was leaving for the United States for good, it wasn't only Madam who was heartbroken.

"But why?" Victor had protested. "Why leave, when you've got everything you could want here?"

"Yes, everything—except the freedom to be myself."

Victor wasn't sure what he felt most—sorrow at being separated from his friend or envy of the searing honesty of his friend's self-knowledge. Peachy had the courage to admit that despite Madam's sponsorship of his talent, which allowed him to reach the height of artistic self-expression, he remained a mere slave to her caprice. When the first rumblings of the fall of the Marcoses echoed beyond the halls of Malacañang, Victor remembered that Peachy had possessed the foresight to see the Marcoses' downfall five years earlier.

Peachy promised he would stay in touch. He did so for a couple of years. But like an old shop sign no one noticed had been slightly fading daily until it became so illegible someone finally took it down, the friends' connection was gone before Victor realized it. He knew he had lost Peachy when, despite his efforts to reach his friend, he didn't receive the usual card or overseas call one Christmas and the following New Year.

℘℘℘℘

Victor splurged on a cab that took him from the airport to the address he'd been given, for he didn't have the slightest idea how to navigate the chaotic traffic of the sprawling foreign city. When he arrived, he was disappointed that no one answered the door of the second-floor unit of a shabby Sunset Boulevard apartment building. It looked more like a seedy motel than a place people called home. Victor wondered whether he had the right location, for he found it difficult to see Peachy living in such shoddy quarters. But he had nowhere else to go. Setting down his luggage beside him, he sat on the concrete floor in front of the apartment's door in the alfresco hallway, determined to wait.

The noise of someone fumbling for keys startled him. He'd apparently fallen asleep, and night had arrived. It was a tall woman, presumably a neighbor, dressed like a teenager in a tight tank top over short shorts. Victor thought she might be a Hollywood has-been or ex-model, with long, bleached, teased hair, leathery tanned skin, and heavy makeup.

"Hi!" she greeted him cheerfully. "Are you waiting for Peachy?"

He sighed with relief and stood. "Yes, yes! Do you know him?"

"You mean her? Sure do." The woman smiled. "We both work at the Chameleon Club. You know . . . down at the Strip?" She had the kind of low, gravelly voice he associated with chain smokers.

"A club? What's Peachy doing there?"

"Didn't you know? She has a fabulous show."

"Show . . . oh, yes, you mean a fashion show?"

"Not that kind. A stage show—you know, singing and dancing?"

Victor was shocked. He'd never thought Peachy would go that far. "Singing and dancing?"

"Yeah. And she's great!" The woman extended her hand. "I'm sorry, I'm Candace. And you are . . . ?"

Her hand was unusually large and firm. "Victor. Peachy and I are old friends. From way back in the Philippines. Just arrived two days ago."

"Oh, my! Then you must be exhausted. But Peachy won't be home until maybe three in the morning. I'm going to the club myself. Would you like a ride?"

Another stroke of luck! "Would you really? That would be most appreciated, ma'am."

She giggled. "Oh, you're such a gentleman. But don't you 'ma'am' me—I'm just Candace! Just give me a minute to change. Would you like to come in?" She stepped into her apartment and turned on a light, holding the door open for him.

"Thank you. You are most kind—Can . . . Candace."

"You bet. Can I offer you a drink?"

"Oh, yes, please." He realized he was not only thirsty—he was famished. His last meal had been an expensive pizza slice that morning at the airport. He couldn't help converting the dollar amounts into peso values in his head, shocked by the prices each time he did.

"Make yourself at home. Pick out something from the refrigerator." She pointed to a portion of the tiny space that passed for a kitchen and retreated into what he assumed was the lone bedroom in the unit.

Candace's hospitality disoriented him. *Americans are too friendly and naive! What if I were a criminal in disguise?* He smirked as he realized many of his countrymen probably considered him exactly that. He got a Coke from the refrigerator, whose meager contents consisted of a carton of orange juice, a near-empty bottle of vodka, and three bottles of beer. He also helped himself to one of three overripe bananas in a basket on the kitchen counter. He sat on the edge of a couch buried under pillows, inching his behind to make space for it. Each pillow was wrapped in fake animal skin or dressed as a cartoon character.

"So how'd you become friends with Peachy?" Candace yelled from inside her bedroom.

"Uh, used to be in business together," he yelled back, quite unconvincingly to himself.

"Yeah? And what business was that?

"Oh, you know—business. Show business." *Well, that's not entirely a lie.*

Just then, Candace came out of her bedroom, struggling to put an earring in one of her pierced earlobes, and walked to where Victor sat. She didn't seem to notice his unease.

"Figures. Filipinos seem to be very artistic people. Great singers and dancers—just like Peachy." She now wore a figure-hugging, rhinestone-studded, purple Mickey Mouse shirt over a black faux leather miniskirt. Victor wondered what Peachy would think of an outrageous outfit like that. While he and his friend both liked modern fashion, they never approved of anything garish or purely trendy. They also deplored the "prosti" look, which was certainly what Candace's style evoked.

Candace finally succeeded in fastening her ludicrously long purple-bead chandelier earrings. "So you and Peachy are old pals, huh? What a surprise Peachy's gonna have. I'd often wondered whether she had any—other friends, that is, apart from me and that SOB Todd."

"Who's Todd?"

"Her old jerk of a boyfriend. He shipped out when a rich old fag spotted him at the club while he was supposedly waiting for Peachy. It didn't take long after the geezer gave him a joy ride in his Porsche before he announced to Peachy he'd had a change of heart. More like a change of fortune is what I call it. But I'm careful not to talk that way about the SOB in front of Peachy. She still has a soft spot for him, ya know? Still hoping he'd come back. So, be forewarned . . . um, sorry, what did you say your name was?"

"Victor."

"Right. So, Victor, are you here for business or pleasure?" Her tone and facial expression turned naughty.

"Oh, I'm just . . . visiting."

"I bet." She winked. "C'mon—let's see Peachy! You can leave your luggage here for now."

She led Victor to the parking lot, where they got into a vintage Mustang. Victor made an effort not to grimace at the fake shaggy tiger-print upholstery that lined not only the car's seats but also the dashboard. "And do you perform too?" Victor asked, to make small conversation. "Like Peachy, I mean." Taking in the stuffed-cloth jumbo dice hanging from the neck of the rearview mirror beside a preserved rabbit's foot, he began to worry about an itch in his throat. It didn't help that Candace's car smelled of stale perfume, hairspray, cigarettes, beer, and something else—something Victor was sure he'd smelled before at many of the parties of Manila's rich and famous. *Why, of course—grass, weed, Mary Jane, pot, or whatever they called the stuff here.*

"Me, perform?" Smiling, Candace offered him a piece of chewing gum. When he refused, she unwrapped it and laid it on her tongue. "No, not yet. But I wish. For now, I just serve the drinks until I perfect the craft, ya know? All of us newbies have to wait our turn until we can prove our stuff. But we all join in the finale number that happens at two o'clock." Between sentences, she made little popping noises with her gum.

As they entered the highway, she pulled out a cigarette from a nearly empty pack in the glove compartment, lit it from the car lighter, and offered it to Victor. When he declined, she stuck it between her lips, the gum still in her mouth. Despite Candace's attempts to blow the smoke out her window, much of it strayed back into the car. Victor suppressed a cough by clearing his throat. He thought of his first attempt, at age eight, to smoke a cigarette. He'd thought the coughing fit would send him to his grave. His mother had laughed and told him it served him right to think himself man enough to try one—which was especially mean because it was she who'd offered him the cigarette in the first place.

Victor noticed some mint candy among the clutter of

little things in a dashboard compartment and asked Candace, "May I?"

"Oh, sure—help yourself!"

eeee

When they arrived at the Chameleon Club, Victor felt he'd been transported to an alien yet fascinating planet. Racy lights that periodically changed colors in green, blue, pink, and purple traced the reptilian shape of a chameleon whose tail was positioned at the bottom end of the facade of the one-story building, looking as though it was crawling diagonally toward the roof.

A long line of carnival Rio dancers, feathered jungle creatures, and Gothic-looking characters turned out to be patrons magnificently arrayed in jewel-colored feathers, faux furs, and sparkling beads, bangles, and baubles, as well as in punk, heavy metal, and new wave fashions. Victor became aware of the shabbiness of his three-day-old travel attire. He yearned for his Don Johnson outfit, but he'd had no room for it in his luggage. He zipped up his jacket to hide the stained cotton shirt underneath, hoping he didn't stink.

The crowd waited impatiently at the front door guarded by a bald Mr. Universe whose high-pitched voice startled Victor. "Whoa there, bitch!" he exclaimed.

"That's all right, Charlie," Candace intervened. "He's with me."

"Oh, okay," Charlie said, allowing them entry before the others. A buzz of protests erupted, which didn't matter because Candace nonchalantly walked right in, pulling Victor with her. She walked so fast that Victor's five-foot-four frame ran to keep up with what he guessed was her six-foot-two.

When they reached the inner sanctum of the club, the lone performer on stage seized Victor's attention. There, basking under a single beam of red spotlight, sizzling amid steamy vapors and curly bands of cigarette smoke, was the most fascinating creature Victor had ever seen. He soon realized to his utter shock that it was none other than Peachy, dressed and looking very much like Liza Minnelli, expertly lip-synching and dancing to the *Cabaret* song that the legendary singer-actress had made famous. The lyrics had never sounded more poignant—especially the part about the futility of crying in one's room.

"Isn't she amazing?" Candace whispered in his ear. Victor could only nod, his gaze fixed upon Peachy. "I've seen her a million times, so enjoy. I'll go ahead. When you're done, just come straight into the dressing room at the back. Peachy and I will meet you there. Don't worry about Jimmy. I'll let him know."

"Thanks." Victor's voice sounded distant to himself, as if the powerful music and its performer had swallowed it. He felt that time itself had stopped. A lump rose in his throat, restricting the oxygen to his lungs, provoking tears of sheer, sweet pain. He barely noticed when the song ended. He was mesmerized by Peachy, by the strangeness of it all, until time seemed to begin again with the audience's rowdy applause and the curtain's fall.

When he'd gathered himself, he looked for the dressing rooms. There was another bouncer at the entrance there, this time a shorter, less muscular hunk with a full mop of dark hair. The man didn't speak, merely stepped aside when Victor introduced himself, which half disappointed him, for he was curious to know whether Jimmy had a high-pitched voice like Charlie.

The dressing room was a small yet brightly lit space illuminated by incandescent bulbs that framed the contours of six oval mirrors—three on each side of the two walls of makeup counters facing each other, reflecting infinite images of the other and making the room seem much larger than it was. Makeup paraphernalia, hairspray, combs, and brushes were heaped upon narrow counters below each mirror. In between were costumes and clothes of every color and variety carelessly strewn about. Clouds of cigarette smoke likewise filled the room, creating a magical setting appropriate for enchanted creatures in different stages of dressing and undressing—Marilyn Monroe, Cher, Donna Summer. Victor glanced twice at Donna, wondering how he'd look dressed up with an Afro that big. He'd only have to grow his hair longer, he imagined.

Candace called out from the back end of the room and waved to him with a big smile. "Hey, Victor, we're over here!" She was changing into a sequined cocktail dress when Victor caught a glimpse of the lump at her groin. Before he could process this discovery, a vaguely familiar face appeared behind her.

CHAPTER 3

As Victor approached, he realized it was Peachy, clad in a red silk kimono. The Liza Minnelli wig was gone, and in its place were stubby little hairs that pierced through the thin-looking skin of his skull like marsh grass struggling to peek above the cracked surface of a dried-up riverbed. No longer was he the beautiful creature on stage, but rather the phantom face of an Edvard Munch painting, devoid of makeup and eyebrows. He held his arms wide open to Victor, smiling, the gleam in his eyes produced by the glint of unshed tears.

"Victor, dahling," he said. "Never in my wildest dreams! Come, come, dear love!" His voice was tired and hoarse like that of a person who was ill.

They hugged, clinging to each other for what felt like eternity.

"Victor, my dear old *chica*." Peachy had barely spoken the last word when he was seized by a coughing spell.

"Oh, look at you—hacking and hemming before your friend!" Candace playfully scolded, handing Peachy a tissue and a water bottle before she returned to her makeup station and gave them the privacy they needed.

After Peachy had sipped some of the water and regained normal breath, he smiled and searched Victor's face before he said, "It finally happened, didn't it?"

"Yes, *bruha*," Victor grinned, while buddy-slapping Peachy on the arm. It had been a long time since he'd had occasion to use the term of endearment for "witch." "It was you who was psychic, after all. The Marcoses are in Hawaii now."

"Never *thee* mind," Peachy replied with a wave of his manicured hand, employing the phrase he used for impossible situations. He sat down in front of a mirror and wiped off remaining makeup from his face.

"I never thought you'd get into this," Victor said. "To think that the most famous Philippine couturier could also make Liza Minnelli look better than Liza Minnelli!"

"Shh! Don't speak of past and forgotten things, *chica*. Nobody here knows that. They only think I can sew my own costumes. They sometimes ask me to do the same for them."

"You mean all these artists are clueless about the true genius among them?"

"They know I'm a genius—just not in *that* way."

They chuckled. It felt so good to laugh with an old friend.

∞∞∞∞

Victor went to live with Peachy after that. He didn't have to ask. They just seemed to pick up where they'd left off, as though they'd never been apart. Peachy curtained off what should have been the living room of the one-bedroom apartment and turned it into Victor's private space.

"Now, let's think of what job we can get you into," Peachy said. "Do you think you could still do the healing stuff?"

Victor shook his head sadly. "The gift has abandoned me. The power used to recharge itself, but in the last few years with the Marcoses, I felt the energy seep out of me until I became nothing but a dried-out broken vessel."

"I'm sorry. I didn't realize it was that bad." Peachy stroked Victor's back as the latter started to cry. "How did it happen?"

Victor blew his nose into the tissue Peachy handed him. "I first felt it when the president was diagnosed with lupus. Madam asked me to cure him, but when I touched him, I felt a viper in my gut coil itself into a knot that blocked off all my energy. I played around for a while, pretending I still had the power, but I couldn't keep it up. Just touching that man fatigued me. Like he'd sucked up all my energy. He kept getting worse—and that's when the Marcos circle closed in on me and isolated me from the First Family. They convinced the Madam that I was all washed up as a healer, that there was no more use for me. That's when they stopped the palace clinic and I had to quickly think of another way to support myself. The Madam's secretary said that due to the loss of donations, there was no way for them to maintain me. They let me keep the townhouse, at least."

"So what did you do then?"

"I diversified into fortune-telling. Faked it. I read palms, decked the tarots, peered into crystal balls, read tea leaves— anything and everything I could get my famous hands on to regain my stature and livelihood. The way the family hid the president's illness from the public worked to my benefit. Their constant denials of his illness maintained my credibility before the people. How could I heal someone who denied he was sick?"

Peachy nodded, smiling grimly.

Victor continued. "All those first years you taught me how to read the personalities around us, remember? That helped a lot—for I learned to see people and the laughable misfortunes they bring upon themselves. The old fools! I became so good at it that even those who had initially lost their faith in me returned. Even the Madam. I got back at them by charging them the most outrageous fees—seven hundred fifty pesos an hour, sometimes a thousand! And they were only too happy to pay it. I was booked from morning to night. Madam was the most pathetic—she needed so much to believe that her family would stay in power forever, believing they were ordained by God, so she always came back just to hear me reassure her. And I did. Especially after Aquino was assassinated. She denied her husband was guilty of all those crimes. She was very good at feigning naiveté and ignorance. She never expressed remorse for spending the people's money to keep up her queen's lifestyle."

Peachy shook his head. "Such a pity. But I'm glad you finally saw their lies, *chica.*"

"Damn right I saw it all. If you ask me, I say everybody deserved what they got—even me, the fake fortune-teller they so willingly trusted. They were so damned naive and stupid. All it took for many of them to get better—at least for a little while—was a little ritual or potion I claimed would heal them of their maladies. The old mind-over-matter trick, you know? Sometimes, I just invented a Latin-sounding incantation—mere gobbledygook, mind you—and they bowed their heads and folded their hands in reverence as if I had cast a magic spell. Those fools!"

Victor laughed and cried hysterically as Peachy patted his heaving shoulders.

ꝟꝟꝟꝟ

Peachy got Victor a job helping the "girls" at the club with their costumes and makeup and sometimes cleaning up after hours. It was a hard life for Victor after the cushy existence he'd lived in Manila. But he had his friend, and that was enough.

It was amazing to Victor the way Peachy lived in America. His apartment was bare, except for the basic furniture and decrepit appliances that had come with it—vastly different from Peachy's almost palatial and impeccably decorated penthouse condominium on Makati Avenue. There seemed to be more medicine in his refrigerator than food. Peachy appeared to have a medication, vitamin, or pill for every ailment known to man. He hardly ate, having almost no appetite, until Victor started cooking some Filipino dishes Peachy had always enjoyed, like *pansit, adobo,* and *sinigang.*

The sole souvenir of Peachy's privileged past in his apartment was an antique three-foot-tall statue of the Nuestra Señora del Santo Rosario that had regally stood in a special glassed-in niche at Peachy's exclusive shop in Makati. The face and hands of Our Lady of the Holy Rosary were made of ivory; her eyes were glass, like the eyes of Victor's little icon of the Black Child Jesus. She wore real teardrop pearl earrings and a robe of pure Mexican silver, hammered and engraved with an intricate design of floral vines and cherubs. Her praying hands reverently held a rosary of filigreed beads of gold. The Marcoses were said to have confiscated the statue from a political foe's ancestral home—raided on the excuse that the family was allegedly hiding and supporting Communist guerrillas. The *santo* had arrived with the Spanish galleons in 1795, a legacy of the family's Castilian forebears.

Victor remembered how Peachy had acquired the priceless statue. After he'd created a fantastic *terno* gown for the Madam, embroidered with twenty-four-karat gold thread, exquisite seed pearls, diamonds, and semiprecious stones, Madam asked him how much he wanted for it. Peachy replied he wanted only one thing: the statue of the Lady he'd always admired in Madam's boudoir. Madam never even blinked, Peachy had said. The next day, she had the statue delivered to his shop by an armored vehicle, with a demand for two more elaborate *ternos* in different colors—for free.

"Three-for-one," Peachy had laughed. The Madam was never to be out-bargained, but the Blessed Mother was worth it, he'd said. The saint was Peachy's muse—as long as he had her, he believed there was always hope.

One late morning, after the evening's hangover had worn off, they were drinking coffee in Peachy's small kitchen when Victor asked, "*Amiga,* what happened all these years—to you, I mean. What've you done with yourself—why live here, like this? You had millions. I escaped with just the shirt on my back, but you were able to transfer all your money and quite a few other valuables from the Philippines, if I'm not mistaken. What happened, my friend?"

Peachy's eyes dimmed with sadness. "What happened is that I fell in love, and *that* kind of love cost me money—a *lot* of money." Peachy told Victor about Todd, an ex-actor who got tired of waiting for roles to come and went for the easy money by prostituting himself to the highest bidder. By the time Peachy realized Todd's true nature, it was too late—he was hooked on Todd, just as Todd was hooked on cocaine and high living. It took only three years for Peachy to use up all of his assets—tens of millions of pesos' worth. He lived with Todd in a Malibu beach house he'd rented at Todd's insistence—until he could no longer afford it. Then they moved to a leased condo in Westlake. For a while, Peachy was still able to support Todd with the Chameleon Club gig and occasional freelance design work from fashion sweatshops. But it was never enough. He'd managed to resist Todd's pleas to sell the *santo,* and, finally, Todd left.

"That was the only time I questioned my judgment," Peachy sighed. "Todd never knew how close I came to selling her in order to entice him back with a new car, a Cartier watch, or some other expensive gift—whatever worked, if only he'd return to me." Peachy believed the Lady had saved him from that foolish act, for he learned just before he was to sell the statue that he had contracted AIDS.

"Yes, *chica,*" Peachy said, smiling. "That's what I have. That's what all those vitamins and medicines in the refrigerator are for. When I think of it, it's somewhat funny how it happened. I got it from a one-night stand, while on the rebound. The guy was a new face in the club, and I flirted with him after a show when I saw Todd with his new boyfriend among the audience. I was hoping to make Todd jealous. Instead, I got myself sick. The joke was on me after all. A few months later, I learned that the guy I'd had a fling with had died of the disease. I was forced to take a test, and the rest is history. It caught up with me fast. A simple chill sends me to the hospital these days."

Victor didn't know what to think or say. When he had left the Philippines, very little was known about AIDS, even among the gay community there. Many deaths were simply attributed to severe flu or pneumonia that usually came with the typhoon, or to tuberculosis, which stalked parts of the crowded and polluted city. Or, in the case of prostitutes and known homosexuals, the deaths were seen as God's punishment for alleged immoral sexual behavior. But in America, there was increasing comprehension of the true nature of the disease, its epidemic proportions, and how one could protect oneself. It perplexed Victor to think of how something like this could happen to his otherwise wise and intelligent friend—until he remembered that Peachy had always had his blind spot: even in America, he was the same old fool for love.

Six months later, as Peachy lay dying, Victor finally took out the Santo Niño from his suitcase, the antique medallion engraved with God's symbols, and the red and white stones from Mount Banahaw. He was thankful he'd brought them along with him. *A miracle could still be possible.*

Victor set up an altar to the Black Child Jesus and lit a pair of candles—one near Peachy's head, the other near his feet. He laid the stones upon Peachy's solar plexus. Then, chanting the incantations and reciting all the prayers he could recall, he touched Peachy's feet, legs, stomach, chest, arms, and forehead with the medallion. He spat into his palms and vigorously rubbed them together, hoping to feel the once-familiar warm throbbing in his gut and the burning sensation on his fingertips that preceded the miracle he used to be able to summon. *Please, please, just this once, again— just for my friend!* he prayed to his Twin Spirit, his eyes awash with tears. He went through the ritual several times, but it was no use. His Twin Spirit had truly abandoned him.

Peachy finally said, "Never thee mind, *chica.*" His voice was very weak, so Victor had to draw his ear close to his friend's lips. "I'm tired. I want to rest now. It was a good life, old chum. A kind of cabaret, wasn't it?" Peachy tried to laugh but ended up coughing. It was more than Victor could bear, and he succumbed to despair, sobbing, until his friend reached for his hand and whispered, "Don't cry, *chica.* I confess—I was the one who was wrong."

"What do you mean, wrong? What are you talking about?" Victor protested, almost angry.

"That people like us, we can't get real love."

Victor remembered the fateful night of their first and last big quarrel. He shook his head.

"Because look, here you are, my friend—loving me! It's more than what some people get. Thank you." With those words, Peachy breathed his last.

Victor found a folded note tucked in the arms of Peachy's Nuestra Señora del Santo Rosario. It said, *For Victor.* Inside, it read, *Take care of my Queen of Angels, chica. She'll watch over you and help you find your own peace and happiness.*

CHAPTER 4

Beep. Beep. Beep. The sound of his pager wakes Victor. He has overslept, and they're calling him. Dinner is now over for the residents, and he's late for his own meal. He rubs his eyes. *Enough of sad dreams for now. They always come back, anyway.*

Through the intercom, he requests a boxed dinner from the kitchen to pick up and eat later in his room. It's time to read to Professor Morrison, the eighty-four-year-old retired literature professor who looks like a Burl Ives Santa Claus. The old teacher doesn't like audiobooks. He wants a live reader, someone with whom he can interact. Victor knows it's companionship the old man seeks more than anything else, just like the other residents—well, almost all. One of the women residents is cantankerous. It's hard for him to see her as ever needing or wanting company of the human kind.

"Good evening, Victor," Professor Morrison greets him in his typical courteous, dignified manner. He's the only one who insists on using Victor's real name. The old man is sitting up in bed, propped against pillows, waiting for Victor to take his usual seat on the bedside chair.

"A good evening to you, too, Professor." He's always more reserved with Professor Morrison than with the other residents. The walls are lined with shelves of books, recalling the somber ambience of the libraries of Father John and Don Hidalgo in Victor's early life. "So, sir, shall we start?"

"Certainly." Professor Morrison nods, more like a salute than agreement.

Victor picks up one of the five volumes on the bedside table. The books are uniformly bound in worn leather that looks almost as old as Professor Morrison himself. He remembers when the professor introduced him to their reading project, *Les Misérables*. The old man pointed to the five volumes, which amused Victor, thinking the professor so eager as to have picked out the next five books they were going to read, until the retired teacher explained all five amounted to just one book.

"Les-mee-se-rab-les?" Victor had asked when he attempted to read the title. Professor Morrison had promptly corrected his pronunciation. Victor commented, "I've heard of it as a Broadway show, but never read it."

"You've never read *Les Misérables*?" Professor Morrison had exclaimed. "The classic story written by your namesake, *Victor* Hugo? Then, my dear boy, it's never too late to start your education."

It always amused Victor whenever Professor Morrison referred to him as a "boy." "Are all the characters *miserable*?" he'd teasingly asked.

Professor Morrison failed to catch Victor's attempt at levity, for he'd responded in his usual serious, teaching voice, "Yes and no. The story does have dark themes, but it ultimately conveys a positive message. It's the story of one man's redemption and another's ruin. It raises large philosophical questions, such as what true justice means for a civilized human society. Should our sociopolitical order, for instance, be anchored mainly on law and the rigid application of such law, under the maxim *dura lex sed lex* that blind Lady Justice represents? Or does being a civilized human society ultimately mean being humane, by accepting the inevitability of human fallibility with compassion? And if so, how could justice and mercy coexist without negating each other?"

"Whoa, Professor! I don't know if I understand all that, but it surely sounds interesting. I don't know, though—this is more than a thousand pages. I've never read a book this long!"

"O, ye of little faith! To paraphrase the old Chinese saying, my boy: To read a thousand-paged book starts with the first page. So, carry on. Carry on! Let's pick up that first volume. Chop-chop!"

After only six weeks, they've read through more than half of the fourth volume. At first, the author's writing style had sounded strange to Victor—a little too formal for his taste, he'd shared with the professor. The latter pointed out that what they were reading couldn't be accurately described as the author's style, as it was an English translation of the original French, and that its tone was as expected for nineteenth-century writing. Victor nonetheless soon became engaged with the story and fascinated by its characters. Monsignor Myriel easily reminded him of Father John, who'd rescued young Victor from what would have been a life of crime. Thus, it was equally easy for him to see himself in Jean Valjean. But the character of Inspector Javert challenged Victor's concept of the righteous man. While he could not find logical fault with the policeman's principled actions, there was something in Javert's rigid style of justice that didn't feel right. Victor had come to appreciate the philosophical questions Professor Morrison raised at the start.

Just as Victor finishes reading the fourth volume, Professor Morrison's snoring tells him he may have lost his listener a few pages ago. The old man's drooping head rises and falls with his labored breathing. Victor checks his watch and is surprised to see it's almost ten. He returns the book to the bedside table, careful to set the fifth and last volume on top of the others as a marker of where to start the next day—unless Professor Morrison should ask him to retrace the last few pages he may have missed. Most of the time, however, the professor does not request this, as he seems to know all his books by heart. Victor sometimes wonders how many times the retired teacher has read each of the books in his collection. They all appear to be well used and loved.

As he positions the old man's head for a more comfortable repose on the pillows, he considers how the last volume might finally bring Jean Valjean face to face with his nemesis, Javert. He can hardly wait to see how it all ends and plans to ask the professor the next day whether he might borrow the fifth volume so he can read it on his own time. After turning off the bedside lamp, he leaves the room quietly.

ℓℓℓℓ

Brenda, who is manning the front desk in the lobby, waves Victor over. "Hey, sistah!" the affable African American woman greets him. "The kitchen sent your dinner here since you forgot to pick it up." She holds up a Styrofoam box.

"Oops! I forgot that I forgot! Thank you, Brenda dahling. And how're things with you?" Victor gives the woman a buss on the cheek. She'd once said she liked it when Victor called her *dahling. It's so Hollywood-ish,* she said, *and you say it so well! You should try auditioning, yourself.* Brenda spends her days auditioning for roles in movies, TV shows, and commercials and her nights working at Casa del Sol to pay her bills. She hasn't had luck landing any substantial roles—just a couple of commercials so far, playing parts so minuscule one can't blink at the risk of missing her entirely.

"Same ol' same ol', and how about you, Tita Vee?" Brenda grins.

"You know me—same young, same young," Victor replies.

Brenda guffaws. "You old fag, you crack me up."

"Always glad to amuse and abuse." Victor smiles. He's never felt the need to correct her assumptions. *It's easier that way.*

"Speaking of abuse," Brenda says, "there's a command here from Mrs. Stanley. She's been driving me crazy demanding new towels in her bath."

"At this hour of the night?"

"Well, yeah. Appears she has trouble sleeping and wants to freshen up, but she says the towels we gave her earlier smell funny. Could you please bring her a new batch? I can't leave the desk, otherwise I'd have done it already."

"Oh, no, dahling. Not old Mrs. Stanley—you know how she hates me!"

"Well, she seems to hate me too. Most everyone, in fact. And there's no one else but you to do it right now. So please, Tita Vee—won't you do it?"

The in-house phone rings. "Front desk, Brenda here. Yes, Mrs. Stanley. No, ma'am. Yes, ma'am. Someone's coming over right now to bring them to you."

She hangs up and looks at Victor with puppy eyes.

Victor lets out a heavy sigh. "Oh, all right. But I'm warning you—I hold you responsible if that old tigress scratches my eyes out."

"I believe we have workers' comp for that." Brenda chuckles.

Victor decides to eat dinner in his room first, hoping the old lady might fall asleep so he can slip in unnoticed and leave the towels. Twenty minutes later, he knocks softly on Mrs. Stanley's door. No one answers, so he turns the knob and walks in. The room is dark except for a night-light shining in the bathroom, the door to which is ajar. *Oh, good, she's fallen asleep.*

He tiptoes in, trying not to make a sound, but he blunders and trips on the leg of a chair near the bathroom door. As he glances up, he sees the glowing porcelain faces of the old woman's antique doll collection staring at him with hollowed-out eyes from behind the glass window of a display cabinet. There is something morbid in their pale countenances—made more frightening by the faint glow of the night-light shining on them.

Victor's heart jumps when a voice suddenly growls, "What? Who . . . who's there?" A bedside lamp turns on, and Mrs. Stanley's scowling face glowers at his ridiculously suspended tiptoeing form. Her long white hair hangs in limp, wiry shreds on both sides of her creased parchment cheeks.

"So, it's you—the nigger and the thief!"

"Excuse me, madam, but what did you just call me?" Anger bubbles in his chest. *How dare this old hag?*

"I called you a nigger—*and* a thief—that's what!" the old woman says venomously. "It's as plain as day—you have black blood in you, don't you? And you're the thief who stole my coins, aren't you?"

"No, I'm not!" Some time ago, the office received complaints from Mrs. Stanley about having lost some of her collection of antique coins. "I had nothing to do with that. And if you please, madam, the subject of my ancestry is none of your business!" Victor reminds himself to go easy and not risk losing his job over the hateful woman. "I was just delivering your towels, so if you can't be nice, Mrs. Stanley,

I'm just going to leave them here." He puts the towels on the chair.

"You'll do no such thing. I'll not wash with anything touched by black hands."

"Then you'll just have to remain the stinky old hag you are, or go to Timbuktu for all I care!" Victor retorts, and leaves Mrs. Stanley's room with his chin held high. He smiles to himself when he realizes that Timbuktu might well be in Africa—*well, it does sound African!*—a good place to exile someone like Mrs. Stanley.

After he steps out and closes the door behind him, something hits and breaks against the other side of it. "Ha! You missed!" he yells. He hears a string of invectives through the door. *Oh boy. Sorry, Brenda—you may have a rough night tonight, but I'm outta here.*

Back in his room, sobriety settles in, then a deep sadness. He buries his face in his pillow. *You have black blood in you, don't you?* He hears the words over and over. *So what if I do, you old hag?* Victor wants to scream back. He ignores the ringing of the intercom phone, followed by his beeper going off. *Oh, deal with it yourselves! I've had enough of her.* But the image in his mind of a hag is now no longer that of Mrs. Stanley. It's his mother. The monster is loose—out to haunt him again. Someone's snatched the key from him and unlocked the dungeon door.

CHAPTER 5

Loretta Vasquez was the eldest of twelve children of a fisher-man and his wife in Zambales province. She was sixteen when she decided she would do whatever was necessary to get herself out of her barrio. She'd had enough of the perennial stink of both fish and babies.

In early 1952, she heard that increasing numbers of U.S. Marine and Navy men were flooding the red-light district of Olongapo City outside Subic Naval Base, seeking rest and recreation from the Korean War. She had an idea. If she could attract at least one of those soldiers, she might earn a one-way ticket to America and leave the squalor of her barrio forever. But first, she had to get herself into the Brown Fox, a bar and nightclub in Olongapo City popular among the *Americanos,* according to her friend Maritess, whose sister Juana was a bargirl in the club. Word was that Juana was engaged to a *Cano,* Danny Boy Olson, the American club owner himself. Maritess said that Danny Boy would soon take her sister to America, and then Juana would send for Maritess. Loretta was determined to get into the club before they left, for she too saw Juana as her ticket to the wonderful world of the *Canos.*

One day, while her mother was hanging clothes on the clothesline outside their home, Loretta slipped into her parents' bedroom and stole the day's fish sales out of the *ataul,* and that same night while the family was asleep, she rode a bus to Olongapo City.

It was almost midnight when Loretta arrived. She walked all the way to the Brown Fox, easy to locate by the thick band of neon lights glowing in an area of the city near the naval base. Beneath a blinking sign that showed a bikini-clad fox with a wagging tail stood three painted women in skimpy dresses smoking cigarettes and rowdily greeting the *Canos* entering and exiting the club. They swayed and jerked their curvy bodies to the beat and rhythm of the loud dance music blaring from inside.

"Hey, Joe—come back soon, okay?" One of them called out to the staggering figures of white-uniformed soldiers. "But bring me some of those PX Marlboros again—or you can't come here no more!" The girls laughed.

"Sure, Babe! See ya!" one of the soldiers replied as his group disappeared into the crowd of patrons in the street.

When Loretta approached them, she realized the women were girls not much older than herself. They only looked more mature because of the makeup they wore. One of them said, "What you want, kid? Scram—you can't be here!"

"I'm looking for Juana."

"No Juana here."

"But my friend, Maritess—Juana's sister—sent me here. I have message for Juana."

At that, the girl nodded to one of the other girls, who briefly left and returned with an older woman who said, "What you want, girl?"

"Juana?" Loretta wasn't sure it was her friend's sister, for when Juana left their barrio, she was thin and dark. This woman was plump and not so dark, with eyelashes so long and makeup so thick, Loretta could barely make out the face behind it.

"No, I'm Jo-Ann now."

"Don't you remember me? I'm Loretta—Maritess's friend?"

"Oh, yes—Loretta! My, you're almost grown up. But what you doin' here? How'd you get here, anyway? It's late!"

"Can I speak with you?"

"C'mon to the back with me."

After Loretta explained what she wanted of Jo-Ann, the older woman said, "Turn around."

Loretta did as she was told. Jo-Ann grabbed her by the chin and examined both sides of the girl's face. "No problem. You'll do all right. You're thin, but that'll change in a month or so here. In fact, you're just in time. We happen to have an opening—one of the girls got sent for by her *Cano*. The lucky *puta* is now living the American life! I'll lend you one of my old dresses—it'll be perfect on you. But we'll have to change your name. 'Loretta' just won't do. We'll call you 'Lorie.'"

Lorie couldn't be happier. She felt she was finally on her way to achieving her American dream. With her face whitened by Chinese pearl cream, her full lips rosy and glistening like a *gumamela* flower—thanks to the stateside lipstick Jo-Ann had lent her—and the few curves of her slim body accentuated by Jo-Ann's slinky old dress, she was convinced she looked prettier, too.

Lorie was surprised to learn that *Americano* referred not only to whites but to blacks as well. Her concept of black men was limited to the *Negritos*, a Philippine aboriginal tribe that lived high up in the Zambales Mountains nearby, known for their dark skin, kinky hair, and very short stature. *Negrito* men still dressed in loincloths, and their women walked around bare-breasted. To Lorie, therefore, the word

Negrito was synonymous with primitive, dirty, and uncivilized. Although the black *Canos* dressed and spoke English like the white *Canos* and were sometimes even taller than the whites, Lorie was not deterred from her conviction that black was ugly and white was beautiful. She decided that if she were ever to have a child it would have to be fathered by a white man or a *mestizo*—a person with some white blood in him—in order to ensure its beauty.

She herself was determined to look as white as possible and often worried she wasn't fair-skinned enough. She was only too willing to believe the older girls when they told her that spreading a white man's semen all over her face resulted in smoother, whiter skin. She didn't understand why the girls laughed when she asked exactly how long it would take for her to look American by doing this. She'd often stared at Jo-Ann, who'd eventually married the fat old *Cano,* and convinced herself that Jo-Ann was positively fairer and prettier than when she had been Juana, the fisherman's daughter.

Lorie disliked her beady, slanted eyes hooded by thick lids, which she blamed on a Chinese great-grandmother. She compensated by drawing on thick black eyeliner to create the illusion of bigger, wider-set eyes like the models she saw in the glossy American magazines some girls got as gifts from their patrons.

It wasn't long before Lorie had a steady clientele, including two *Canos*—one black, one white. The *Negro,* Doug, was the first black American man she'd seen who was tall. He fascinated her, but she was quite sure she didn't want to have anything to do with him. She pronounced Doug's name like she'd say the English word for canine. As far as she was concerned, there was only one thing that distinguished

Doug from a *Negrito*—his height. Even the name for them sounded similar: *Negro, Negrito.* It was all the same to her.

Lorie wanted, rather, Doug's white buddy with the blond hair—a guy named Mike—who didn't look much older than she. Mike had a lanky frame and acne. She knew what to do the first time Mike paid to have the privilege of her company all night.

She wasn't an innocent concerning the mechanics of sexual intercourse. Her parents' bedroom had a curtain for a door and was separated from the children's sleeping area by mere woven bamboo walls. She could easily hear their mating noises, and the sea breeze blew the curtain far enough for her to witness all she needed to see. She practiced on Pedro, the boy next door, in her father's *bangka* down at the beach one summer night. After they'd finished, she rinsed in seawater, careful to get her fingers in there, washing out the sticky juices. She'd overheard the local *comadrona*—the midwife who'd helped deliver all her mother's children— explain to her mother that this was a cheap, simple way to prevent pregnancy.

But with Mike, she didn't need to do that. If she got pregnant, all the better, for then she'd have an American baby—her passport to América. So she drank, flirted, and danced with Mike all night, and when they both tired of that, she allowed him to take her into the Brown Fox's special discount rooms. But she hadn't counted on Doug. Deep into the beer-fuddled night, when she thought she'd dreamt of Mike going at it again with her, Doug joined in the fun. She screamed when she found both men naked beside her in the morning.

During her months of pregnancy, she prayed it would be

Mike's baby. It was because of that hope that she didn't have an abortion. But when the day finally came, she gave birth to a black baby boy, her very own *Negrito*.

As a young child, Victor would cry when Lorie yelled at him, "Get away from me, *Negrito*! Get away from me, you sorry excuse for a boy! You freak! *Putang ina mo!*" When he was older, such outbursts from his mother only made him laugh. The last words literally meant, "Your mother is a whore." For once, his mother told him the truth.

During those years with his mother, Victor wished God had been more generous to him. If only the Creator had arranged for him to have been instrumental in giving his mother a visa to America, despite his being black, she might have been kinder to him. But neither Mike nor Doug ever returned to the Brown Fox. It was said both men were killed in Pyongyang the month Victor was born, their bodies blown to bits.

Jo-Ann never made it to America. Old and obese Danny Boy suffered a heart attack while she was very diligently performing her wifely duties on him. It was a pity, for it turned out Danny Boy still had a wife in America whom he'd never divorced. The U.S. Embassy refused to accept Jo-Ann's Philippine marriage certificate. "How could years of living with a man and servicing him as a wife not count for anything with these *Canos*?" Jo-Ann had wailed. But it was futile to continue crying over spilled rice.

And so practical Jo-Ann did the next best thing: she took over the Brown Fox. She became Big Mama for all the Brown Fox girls. And she took the "big" part of her name quite literally—for she grew and grew and grew, as though mimicking the late Danny Boy, until she was three hundred pounds on a five-foot-two frame. Jo-Ann's younger sister,

Maritess, also grew tired waiting for her sister to bring her to America. She ended up marrying Pedro instead, and got pregnant every year.

Most of this story—his mother's history, his own origins—Victor had learned from his godmother, his *Ninang* Jo-Ann. The rest he'd imagined.

On his tenth birthday, beaten black and blue yet again by his mother because he'd failed to serve her morning beer on time, Victor ran away. His *Ninang* Jo-Ann gave him ten pesos as a birthday gift and told him to get as far away as he could from that place, to forget where he came from, to make something of himself, and most of all, to forget the woman who'd given birth to him. Lorie was on her way out anyway, a woman for whom the Brown Fox no longer had any use. No customers would touch Beer-Breath, as they called her, and she was often comatose.

CHAPTER 6

Allowing memories of his mother to invade his thoughts was like opening Pandora's box. Victor remembered all the bad things that had happened to him after he left Subic Bay. He remembered how the police threw him into Manila City Jail after he was caught shoplifting an apple in Chinatown—an act of desperation to appease his hunger. He remembered how he was raped by the adult inmates and forced to do despicable things. It was there where he'd discovered the other reason why his mother hated him so much.

Apparently, he was made differently from normal human beings. He was neither male nor female, for he had the anatomy of both genders. He hadn't known any names for it—he learned those later. He hadn't understood that what he had was not quite a penis, but more likely an enlarged clitoris, and that his scrotum was formed like a labia that the men in jail mistook for a vagina. They'd violated him everywhere they could penetrate him, his unusual anatomy shocking the scoundrels at first before they celebrated their good fortune by having a go at him at various hours of the day and night. Victor learned to survive by simply submitting. Some of the men compensated him with biscuits or fruit their visiting relatives brought them, but not one of those half-humans dared get in the way of the hardened beasts who'd often required full satisfaction from him.

When he was released from jail, he would go for days without a decent bite to eat. He discovered that by allying himself with street-gang kids, he had access to plenty of glue and varnish to sniff, which helped him forget his hunger and pain. He paid his dues by pickpocketing with the gang and allowing the older, bigger boys to have their way with him.

He remembered the cold, wet nights, the struggle to claim shelter under the bridges during typhoon season. It was enough to make him want to go back to jail, where at least he got fed. He remembered seeing boys and girls his age going to school with clean uniforms and colorful lunch boxes, their parents not far behind them or picking them up at day's end. God, how he'd hated them.

One day, when another raging typhoon had crowded the undersides of bridges with the scum of the city, he was forced to look for a dry spot elsewhere. He had wandered off into a part of the metropolis he'd never explored before and noted a chapel on a side street, locked for the night. He was soaked through and shivering to his core.

The inviting crimson glow of vigil candles reached out to him, promising him warm, dry relief. He threw a rock to break one of the chapel's glass windows, and having accomplished that, reached in to unlatch the lever to open it and sneak in. He grabbed the altar tablecloth, wrapped himself with it, and lay in a fetal position on a bench before the smiling statue of a woman holding her little son close to her exposed heart. A tray of flickering candles inside ruby-colored glass votives pleaded with their last flames for a litany of lost causes before the mute saints. A deep, abiding blackness overcame him, until the whole world became nothing but a warm cocoon of forgetting.

He awakened to someone shaking him roughly. *"Hoy, hoy!"* a young man said. "Wake up! You can't stay here. Go away before I call the *Padre* and he calls the police. You're the one who broke the window, aren't you? Aren't you?"

Victor tried to speak and open his eyes, but he couldn't. He felt as if his eyes were sewn shut. He wanted to say, *Yes, please, call the police so they'll bring me back to jail,* but his throat had dried up from the same burning sensation that welded his tongue to the roof of his mouth. His whole body seemed on fire, and he couldn't move. His arms and legs felt heavy like metal. Indeed, his mouth tasted like metal.

After a few minutes, he heard the young man's voice again, joined by that of an older man. "Here he is, *Padre.* I can't wake him."

Large hands touched his forehead before peeling away the tablecloth from his body. The older man cried, "Good God! This boy's burning up! Carlos, come, help me carry him into the infirmary." He spoke English, this much Victor was sure—he'd learned some English from the *Canos* in Subic. But the man spoke it with a strange sound, different from the *Americanos.*

When Victor regained consciousness, he was being attended to by the older man who looked like a *Cano* but was not a *Cano.* Father John was a Dutch priest of the Missionaries of the Sacred Heart. The mission ran a small Catholic school for boys in the city. When the priest asked him what his name was, he couldn't remember it. He told the priest he was just *Itim,* "the black one," to his fellow street scavengers. He said he was an orphan.

"Not to worry," the priest said. "Here, you've found your family at last."

Father John told him he'd almost died of pneumonia but that God had saved him because maybe Victor still had an important mission to fulfill in life. For himself, said the *Padre*, he believed God had brought Victor to him that he might teach and guide the boy toward the righteous life.

When Victor had recovered, Father John offered him the chance to live and work with him at the school. They were sharing lunch one day when the priest suggested it. Victor could think only of the bowl of steaming soup before him. He remembered all the hungry nights and days. He looked at Father John's kind, pale-blue eyes and immediately said yes.

Father John then quickly organized a baptismal ceremony in which he christened him Victor Mariano. "'Mariano,'" the priest explained, "to symbolize your adoption as a son of the Blessed Mother and therefore brother to our Lord Jesus. And 'Victor' so that in Mary and Jesus you will be victorious in all the trials of your life."

After the baptismal ceremony, when they were alone, Father John looked intently at Victor and placed his hands on the boy's shoulders. "Victor, when we found you, I asked a doctor to come and check on you. He had to give you a complete physical examination to find out what was wrong with you. Do you know what he discovered? Aside from your pneumonia?"

Victor remained silent, trembling, afraid the priest would tell him what he already knew: that he was a freak just like his mother had told him many times, just like all those men at the jail had made him realize.

The priest smiled as he answered his own question. "There

is absolutely nothing wrong with you, Victor! You are perfect as you are, just as God made you."

Victor did not understand what he felt then, for he had never known what it was to feel accepted. When later he would look back on this time, he would remember it as the first time he felt absolutely loved.

As Father John's ward, he lived in a dormitory on school grounds and worked with the priest and the young seminarians who trained there as part of their initiation for the priestly and missionary life. Before and after school hours, Victor swept floors, assisted Father John as sacristan during Mass service, mowed the lawns, and helped the cook with the marketing and cooking. It was there that he learned how to make all the delicious Filipino dishes that Peachy would later enjoy.

During school hours, Father John insisted Victor attend classes. Though he was twelve years old, he had to start in the first grade, where he again became the object of cruel jokes and teasing by the other students. The children called him names like "overgrown *Negrito*" or "fat *bakla*." His rotund physique thankfully masked the female-looking breasts that had begun to form on his chest. He resolved to bear his classmates' insults quietly, for compared to the harsh street life he'd had to endure, life with Father John was heavenly.

It didn't take long for Victor to advance into the higher grades, even skipping some. He had a natural acumen for learning, according to the priest, who seemed very pleased with his progress. This made Victor happy with an abiding joy that differed from the intoxicating yet fleeting ecstasy he'd felt when he'd first arrived in the streets of Manila, dizzy with overwhelming freedom.

One day, Father John called him to the library and showed him a book that contained a picture of what looked like an old painting on a broken piece of stone wall. The priest told him it had been found in an archeological site in a country called Italy. The image was of a peculiar creature with female breasts and the genitals of a man. *Just like me!* Victor looked up at the priest inquiringly.

"Do you know who this is?" Father John asked.

Victor shook his head.

"Hermaphroditus. The ancient Greeks believed him to be a demigod, the child of Aphrodite, the goddess of love, and of Hermes, the messenger of the gods. Those who worshipped him believed him capable of curing all human beings' illnesses, except his own. This is what others call someone like you, Victor—a hermaphrodite. But unlike Hermaphroditus, by God's grace, you will be capable of healing whatever ails you. You have everything in you that you'll ever need to face your challenges in life. Just remember to stay true to yourself, my son."

Later, Peachy would further explain to Victor how it was entirely possible that a man could really be a woman inside, no matter his anatomy—just like Peachy himself, who not only loved to dress as a woman but also desired only men. "By the way, *chica,* you wouldn't happen to have the power to give me a woman's body, would you?" Peachy once asked Victor in a half-joking, half-serious tone.

"I'm afraid not, my friend," Victor replied. He couldn't alter even his own anatomy.

"Oh, too bad. Well, perhaps when I've saved enough money, I'll go to America and get myself fixed." Peachy said he was following transgender medical research and treatments being developed in the United States that could turn him into a real woman.

Victor wasn't sure what compelled him to say and do what followed next. Perhaps he'd already been secretly thinking it, but the words and actions got out before he could stop himself. He glared at Peachy and said, "Get yourself *fixed*? But what is a real woman—or man, really?"

"What do you mean, *chica*?"

"I mean, what do you think makes a man a man, and a woman a woman? Is it our bodies? Do we have to be one or the other? Can't we just love another person, regardless of the parts we were born with?"

"*Ai, chica,* you're not making any sense now. What the heck are you talking about? Are you drunk or high or something?"

"I'm serious, Peachy! For instance, what and who would you say I am?" At that, Victor completely undressed before the shocked Peachy—which was priceless, because Peachy was not one to be easily shocked. "Am I man or woman?"

After gasping, hand over mouth, eyes big as billboards, and speechless for what seemed forever, Peachy exclaimed, "Oh my God. Victor, I'm not sure whether to hate you for already having the parts I want for myself, or adore you for being a . . . a goddess!" He then knelt before the naked Victor and bowed, arms worshipfully rising and falling, inciting both of them to break into riotous laughter.

When they'd settled into sobriety, Peachy said, "I've only heard of people like you as mythological creatures. I'd no idea you really existed—and yet here you are: no more extraordinary than being a friend to someone like me." Peachy hugged Victor, making Victor feel again what he'd first felt when Father John told him, *You are perfect as you are, just as God made you.*

The rapping on his door snatches Victor from the past. *Shit. Time to face the music.* He turns on the bedside lamp and sees it's past midnight. Reluctant to get up from his cot, he drags his feet to the door. When he opens it, he sees Brenda, her round shoulders rising and falling from breathlessness.

"Hi, Tita Vee. May I come in?"

"Sure." Victor's reply is glum. He opens the door only wide enough to allow Brenda to enter. She looks around the small room, unsure where to seat herself. He motions for her to take the wooden stool by his cot.

Victor sits on the edge of his cot, arms folded on his lap, ready for a scolding.

"I only have a few minutes. Nurse Ilana volunteered to man the front desk for me for a short while." Brenda's tone is careful, like she's afraid she might step on eggshells with every word she speaks.

Victor nods.

"Tita Vee, what happened between you and Mrs. Stanley? I'm sorry, but I have to know before I complete an incident report. Mrs. Stanley riled us good out there. Said you acted real terrible and insulted her. Said you called her a hag and told her to get lost. To Timbuktu?" Brenda smiles as though saying, *Way to go, Tiger,* but she soon resumes her serious expression.

"Ilana had to administer a tranquilizer. I'm your friend— you know that. So I want to be fair to you as much as possible. I know that Mrs. Stanley is an especially difficult person, so I'm sure there's another side to this story."

"It really doesn't matter, Brenda," Victor replies. "You can write whatever she told you. I'm not sure I'm even right for this job anymore."

"Don't go to extremes. Everyone loves you. Well, almost everyone." Brenda smiles.

Victor refuses to be cheered. "She called me a nigger."

"I'm sorry to hear that. I know she has that habit when she's pissed, and it's got to stop. Don't worry, I'll take it up with Mrs. Fernandez. Maybe she can talk to her or her family."

"Oh, no need to make a fuss over me. She's not entirely wrong, you know. About me, I mean. I want to show you something."

Victor opens a drawer from his bedside table and pulls out a yellowed and creased envelope. It bears the name of the boy who died in the streets of Manila a long time ago and was reborn as Victor Mariano. The return address is that of his *Ninang* Jo-Ann. She mailed it to him at the seminary after he'd sent her a brief note thanking her for the ten pesos she had given him, telling her he was about to graduate from high school and was on his way to becoming somebody. He'd never even inquired about his mother. His godmother wrote back to tell him that Lorie had died from alcohol poisoning not long after he'd left. *God rest and forgive her soul, just as I hope you'll be able to forgive her, for your sake,* she wrote. But he never could, never did. *I hope she burns in hell,* he'd said to himself when he read the letter and stared at the photo that came with it. But he cried as well, like a little boy who'd lost his mama.

"Here, Brenda. This is who I really am."

Brenda looks puzzled as she takes the black-and-white photo from Victor's hands. He understands her confusion. It shows a young, smiling, Asian-looking girl wearing a spaghetti-strap dress, her thin brown arms locked possessively around the scant shoulders of a similarly young, shy-looking Caucasian man in a Hawaiian shirt. On the other side of the girl stands another young man likewise wearing a Hawaiian shirt, big, black, with thick lips twisted into a self-assured smile and fingers flashing the victory sign. The group is seated at a table laden with beer bottles.

"What's this?" Brenda asks.

"That, my dear, is the bitch who gave birth to me, the man who should've been my father, and the guy who ended up being him, instead."

"I'm sorry. Must have been that bad, huh?" Brenda looks embarrassed before her eyes light up. "But look on the bright side. Like this black guy here—he's your daddy?"

"Yes."

"I'd sometimes wondered, but was shy to ask. Why, you aren't simply Filipino, then. You really *are* also a bro! And that's the bright side of all this," Brenda declares, smiling.

"You can call me that, I guess." Victor remains glum. "But Mrs. Stanley isn't too far off, either."

"That's not true! It's not right, and no one has the right to use that word, Tita Vee. I understand why you reacted the way you did. It's not acceptable." Brenda lays a consoling hand on Victor's shoulder. "Apart from that, don't take Mrs. Stanley too personal, or she'll drive you crazy! You already know she hates everyone who looks black. Only, she's more careful with me because she knows I'm practically evening management."

"What can I say, dahling? It sucks down the food chain!" Victor finally smiles.

Brenda chuckles. "It's nice to see you smile again. But just the same, it's not acceptable—and I'd say, not even lawful! —for her to say the N-word," Brenda declares. "Don't worry, Tita Vee. I'll take care of this."

He expects her to leave, but she continues, "And do you know another reason why Mrs. Stanley hates us so much? And I mean, it's not just that we're black and she's nothing more than a sad, old, racist woman?"

"What?"

"Because her great-great-granddaddy sired several chicka-dees with some of his slave gals back in the ol' plantation days—something the women in her family vowed never to forgive, especially after the black family line sued her genera-tion for their share of the plantation. Can you imagine that? Never was such a case heard of, and the first court agreed to allow the case to proceed until a higher court overturned its decision. But still. The descendants of the ol' masters considered it the ultimate insult."

"How do you know all this?" Victor asks, eyebrows raised.

Brenda flashes a naughty smile. "Oh, it's just the usual mouse-versus-cat game—we mice know them cats. Just as much as they can sniff us out, we can sniff them out, too." Brenda winks. "Actually, it was all over the papers years ago. There were rumors that what led the higher court to dismiss the case was fear that the black descendants of President Jefferson might do the same, and then what would that do to the whole establishment, let alone American history, right? The case's dismissal is what's partly feeding the black reparations movement now."

"You serious? An American president had black kids?" Victor exclaims.

"Sure thing! He had them with his slave gal, Sally Hemings. It's been a long known secret among us black Americans, but it's becoming public now. Yeah, I know—right? The author of the Declaration of Independence, of the right of men to liberty, had problems freeing his own slaves."

Victor is amazed at Brenda's knowledge. *She's not just a nice, good-looking wannabe actress, after all.* The phone rings. This time, he answers it. "Victor here. Hi, Ilana. Yes." He turns to Brenda. "It's for you."

"Yes, Ilana?" Brenda answers. "Oh, no! When? We'll be right there!" She returns the receiver. "Tita Vee, I'll need you at the front desk. Seems like everyone has trouble sleeping tonight. Professor Morrison fell in his bathroom. Hit his head. Lucky he was able to push the emergency button. Gotta go—an ambulance is on its way!"

"But . . ." is all Victor can utter. He wants to say, *Let me fix him.* His fingers instinctively touch the etched engravings on the ancient medallion he wears under his shirt. He wants to help his friend and rush to his aid like Brenda, but he realizes he is powerless. Why he still wears the now-useless accessory, he's not sure. *Old habits die hard. How slow the mind is to adjust to new realities!* His gift had abandoned him a long time ago—the bitter consequence of his betrayal. But sometimes he feels it's just hiding somewhere inside him, only waiting for him to find the right key to free it from its prison.

Victor can only follow Brenda and watch helplessly as the paramedics wheel away Professor Morrison's unconscious body.

CHAPTER 8

It was during a Sacred Heart School field trip to Mount Banahaw that Victor received the gift of healing. He was fifteen years old and, in many ways, still very much a child who'd miraculously hung on to an innocence that allowed him to appreciate with wonder and curiosity the world Father John introduced to him. He consumed knowledge as though he had been famished too long and was just now served a feast. But the first twelve years of his life outside the sheltered confines of the seminary school had also made him older and wiser than many youths his age. All these qualities made him ripe for a particular calling—though not the calling the Catholic priest hoped he'd choose.

The guide who accompanied Father John and his students up the mountain said that Mount Banahaw was an active volcano. It was also called Vulcan de Aqua because of the many natural springs that flowed from it. Local residents considered the mountain sacred and its spring waters holy because of their healing properties. Other sites, including caves and caverns, were likewise believed to have curative powers. These locations were said to have been revealed to a man named Agripino Lontoc by the Santong Boses, or "Holy Voices," during the Spanish colonial era. Many religious sects had thus established themselves there.

It was easy for Victor to understand this. The surreal beauty of the majestic mountain, whose three peaks were constantly blanketed by mist and clouds—along with its whispering streams, mysterious caves, breathtaking waterfalls, and canopied forests—lent an undeniable mystical quality to the place. He sensed that the mountain was indeed home to a great and benevolent spirit, a supernatural force that evoked the very power of the Creator of the universe, a soul older than any soul. He didn't know how he'd discerned this, but when he stepped on the red, loamy soil, he felt as though he were walking on hallowed land.

In contrast, his classmates found fodder for mischief. When they knew Father John and the guide weren't looking, they teased Victor. "Hey, Victor, say hello to your family!" they laughed, pointing to a group of monkeys watching from the branches of old *balete* trees. The boys then followed Victor around, mimicking the animals' cries and behavior. Victor ignored them, refusing to be distracted from the enchantment of a place that seemed at once both strange and familiar to him, as though he had been there before but had forgotten. Only when the guide caught the boys jesting and warned them of lightning suddenly striking the irreverent did they cease their taunting.

The group entered the mountain trail through Pintong Lihim—the Secret Door—past gigantic, moss-covered boulders and rows of ancient trees twisted and bent low, as if kneeling before goddess Mother Earth herself. Victor saw in the shadows the vigilant eyes and serene countenances of sages, the tormented faces of restless souls, and the monsters that forever bedeviled them. They followed him in the facade of rocks and stones that jutted out of the mountainside or peeked above the foliage of flirty ferns, swaying palms, pliant bamboo, and slithering vines. He heard the songs of nymphs in the flowing crystal waters of the mineral springs, whispering their secrets to him as he and his companions satisfied their thirst from the pebbled banks and washed themselves clean of the prickly heat and humidity. He heard the cries of crows and maya birds call out to him, "Be worthy! Be worthy!" Then, at the crest of Santong Durungawan— the Holy Window—Victor felt he'd glimpsed heaven itself through the view of clear, blue, open sky. There, the air was cool and refreshing at last, as though they had reached a different clime altogether.

It was when they arrived at the sanctuary offered by Kweba ng Dios Ama, the Cave of God the Father, that the miracle happened. Father John offered Mass in celebration of the culmination of their journey. During the consecration of bread and wine into the sacred body and blood of the Christ, Victor heard the wind spirit sing its song of praise in crescendoing strains of *Holy! Holy! Holy!* echoing through the cavernous rock cathedral before he felt a fierce stream of light, heat, and energy pass through his body, seizing him completely. The majestic columns of stalagmite and stalactite spun around him in a vertiginous spell, ending in a blackness more complete than he'd ever known. His last vision was of the smiling statue of the Blessed Mother holding the God-Child in her arms, just as he'd seen her at the Sacred Heart Chapel a few years back.

Later, Father John would fill in Victor with what happened while he was unconscious. A savage storm appeared out of nowhere after Victor fell into a coma from an inexplicable fever. It prevented the group's descent, so they all had to remain at the cave while the guide left to get help from a small village midway down the mountain. High up in those dense forests, no doctor could be found save for a local *arbolario,* an old man versed with the ancient healing art of herbs, potions, and incantations. Were it not for Father John's fear of his young charge dying before the storm had passed, he said, he'd not have allowed the native healer to perform his otherwise heretical magic on Victor.

Father John recounted how the *arbolario* started by boiling water in a small clay pot over a pit fire. Then the old man lit a pair of candles and placed one each at Victor's feet and head. In a bowl carved out of stone, he burned aromatic herbs that filled the cave with their tranquilizing incense. After that, he wiped Victor's face and body—first, with a washcloth dipped in what the old man described as consecrated water from one of the mountain's mineral springs; then, with consecrated coconut oil. He placed two smooth stones—one red and one white—over Victor's abdomen at a spot Victor would later learn was the site of the solar plexus. The stones, the *arbolario* explained, were pebbles taken from two streams that flowed from a mysterious source inside the mountain: the red one, Tubig na Dugo, or Blood Water; and the white one, Tubig na Gatas, or Milk Water. He said they believed these were manifestations of the blood and water that came out of the pierced side of the Christ.

Father John continued to describe the ritual of the native healer. The *arbolario* blessed various parts of Victor's body with a medallion engraved with strange symbols and characters, all the while murmuring prayers and incantations alien to the ears of the Catholic priest, although they sounded Latin. The healer would later show Victor that the circular medallion was engraved with the all-knowing, all-seeing "Eye of God," an eye enclosed within a triangle. Each of the triangle's angles was punctuated with symbols representing the three persons of the Holy Trinity: a fish for God the Son, a dove for God the Holy Ghost, and a burning bush with twin tongues of fire swirling around each other for God the Father-Mother. Inscribed on the other side of the medallion were the Latin words, *Veritas Vos Liberabit.* The truth shall set you free.

When the ritual ended, Father John said, Victor startled everyone when he suddenly sat up, eyes glazed, as though awakened by the roaring thunder. The *arbolario* laid him back gently on the makeshift blanket of banana leaves spread out on the bare earth. Then, dropping some herbs in a cup made from half a coconut shell, he poured boiling water over them, creating a kind of tea. He made Victor drink the liquid and laid him back on the banana leaves. After a few minutes, the old man called for Father John to come forward and feel Victor's forehead. Father John said he was amazed to find Victor's fever completely gone. He later admitted to Victor that, while he was perplexed by witnessing someone who was not exactly a follower of traditional Catholic—let alone Christian—doctrine and practice possessing the power to summon a miracle, he also conceded there was much in God's universe he was still learning.

Victor rested with everyone in the cave through the night and woke up the next morning asking, "What happened?" The other boys groaned and whined. They complained about mosquito bites and ghosts, and pleaded that they be allowed to go home. The old man warned Father John that Victor was not yet strong enough to make the hike down the mountain, suggesting he leave Victor with him until the boy had fully recovered his strength. He told the priest not to worry, assuring him Victor was in good hands, and that he considered it his sacred trust to keep the boy safe and well. Father John hesitated, but seeing how Victor was indeed still weak, agreed. He promised Victor he'd be back in a couple of days with a doctor.

It took Father John not two, but forty days to get back to his young charge. Extraordinary rain and thunderstorms that persisted throughout those six weeks seemed to conspire with the mountain to keep Victor there. By the time Father John recovered Victor, the *arbolario* had already taught the boy what he needed to know about himself, to understand he had a special calling. Victor also learned that he had a Twin Spirit from the spirit world that was his special channel into that world—a soul mate who enabled him to access the powers latent in him.

Victor returned home with Father John but stayed only long enough to finish high school. The summer after his graduation, he bid his father-mentor good-bye. The priest was very sad to see him go. He said he didn't want Victor to leave, but he had seen for himself how, with Victor's simple touch, ailments such as a classmate's stomachache, bad gash, fever, or toothache immediately disappeared. "I don't understand this gift God has given you, my son," Father John had said, "but it is obvious He has given you something special. I cannot presume to know how to teach you to use it in the way you are meant to, so I have no choice but to let you go. But remember that wherever you find God, my son, I am there with you also."

Priest and protégé then hugged like father and son. It was the last time Victor saw his foster father. He later learned that when Father John became afflicted with liver cancer, the Sacred Heart Mission sent him back home to the Netherlands, where he died. Victor wished he had been able to help his mentor, but he was nowhere near ready at that time to cure the disease of the man he'd loved as a father.

For three years, Victor apprenticed with his new teacher, the *arbolario* at Mount Banahaw. The old man taught him how to harness the power that the Lord of the Mountain had given him. Victor watched and learned as he witnessed how the old man surgically excised, using only his fingers, all types of abnormal growths inside people's bodies—tumors, gallstones, even fish bones lodged in people's throats. He learned how to stop internal bleeding and straighten and mend broken bones. The *arbolario* often accomplished these procedures without significant loss of blood from the patient. Soon, Victor also began performing minor cures among the locals in and around the mountain under the *arbolario's* tutorship.

The time came for Victor's Purificacíon, his baptism in the waters of the mountain's Spring of Life, the Tubig ng Buhay. As the *arbolario* conducted the part of the rites where he lowered Victor under the water, Victor sank in the shallow water and could not get up. The old man had to pull him up, and after having revived him, told him, "*Hijo,* the Lord of the Mountain accepts you fully as His son, but there is a stone in your heart that keeps you from reaching the full promise of your gifts. For this reason, prophesy shall not come easy to you until such time when you shall have rid yourself of this stone's dark spell. Nonetheless, you will be a great healer. Your gift for healing will abide with you for many years. But a time of reckoning will come when you will have to cast this stone away or risk sinking with it. When that happens, I won't be there to save you. You will have to save yourself—by healing yourself."

Victor could guess what the stone in his heart was, but the *arbolario* did not speak of it again. "Only those ready to hear the truth hear it," he often heard the old man say.

After Victor had learned all the *arbolario* could teach him, they parted ways. The old man's last words to him were, "Be careful, *hijo,* to use your gifts only for good. Never throw your pearls to swine. Above all, never use them for your own glory or for evil, lest you lose them." The *arbolario* gave him his own medallion with God's sign on it, along with a set of pebbles from the Spring Waters of Blood and Milk.

"Name your *Padrón,* my son," the old man asked during Victor's confirmation rites before the secret assembly of their brethren that consisted of both male and female consecrated healers.

"I choose," Victor solemnly replied, "El Negro Santo Niño de Jesus." He had discovered his Twin Spirit was the spirit of the Black Child Jesus who spoke to him with the voice of a little boy, often playful, yet always wise and compassionate.

Victor went on to perform great miracles in the name of the dark-skinned Child-God.

CHAPTER 9

"I understand how Mrs. Stanley must have angered you," Mrs. Fernandez, the retirement home manager, says in a clipped tone. "But it's not within your rights as an employee here to act on your emotions concerning our residents, Tita Vee."

The first time Victor had heard Mrs. Fernandez's name was when the Casa del Sol owners instructed him to report to the manager by a certain date. He'd wondered whether Mrs. Fernandez was Filipino, "Fernandez" being a common Filipino surname. But then there were also many Hispanics and Latinos in California who had Spanish-sounding surnames like most Filipinos do. When he finally met her, she even looked like one—with her short stature, brown complexion, slightly slanted, dark eyes, and straight black hair. So he'd feared she might know him and worried he'd lose his new job. The Filipino community was a closely connected and gossipy circle, after all, even in America. But when Mrs. Fernandez opened her mouth, she immediately betrayed her Mexican heritage, much to Victor's relief.

He stares at his folded hands. "Yes, Mrs. Fernandez. I'm very sorry."

"If you have a complaint about the way you've been treated, then report it to management—don't take it out on the person. Our residents are in varying stages of old age, senility, even dementia. This means tolerating them with understanding and compassion. This is exactly our business as a senior assisted-living home."

"Yes, ma'am."

"We don't want any more trouble from Mrs. Stanley. Her family is very influential, as you know. There may be no other chances for you if something happens between you and her again."

"I understand, Mrs. Fernandez."

"All right, carry on with your duties."

"Thank you, ma'am."

"Oh, one more thing, Victor."

"Yes, Mrs. Fernandez?"

"Professor Morrison wanted you to have this while he's in the hospital."

Victor instantly recognizes what she hands him. It's the last volume of *Les Misérables*. He didn't have the chance to ask for it, but here it is.

"He says for you to catch up on your reading." Mrs. Fernandez's face finally stretches into what looks like a smile.

"Thank you, ma'am. And how is the professor?"

"He's fine—just a concussion. But he'll have to stay there a few days for observation. At his age, it could have been fatal."

Victor nods and quietly slips out of the manager's office, clutching the book.

I almost blew it this time. How could I have let that Mrs. Stanley get to me?

Wondering how he might avoid the grumpy old woman from then on, he sighs as he proceeds toward the storage room. There, he deposits the book on an upper shelf and retrieves the janitorial cart.

The hallways need cleaning again today. He has been up since dawn, working the main floor hallways and visitors' bathrooms. Now, he just has to mop the second floor. After mixing another batch of water, vinegar, and Lysol in the huge pail installed in the cart, he heads for the elevator. Some of the residents are still in bed, although a few are already having breakfast at the dining pavilion. It's a manageable time to clean the floors.

Right. Left. Right. Left. Thus goes the almost hypnotic sweeping motion of his mop. Gripping the handle, his hands are bare, callused, and dry. Worker's hands. There was a time when they were soft, manicured, and pampered with grateful kisses and gem-encrusted rings. A privileged man's hands. More important, they used to be a healer's hands, like the hands of Father John and the *arbolario* that had brought Victor back to life.

Father John was the biggest, tallest man Victor had ever seen—taller than any of the *Americanos* he'd met. His hands were equally large, almost disproportionate to his arms. But Father John's hands always served, whether it was to consecrate the body and blood of the Savior, write letters to friends and benefactors, care for fevered boys and feed them warm soup, or turn the pages of the Holy Book to read to ignorant youth like him.

Once, while Father John was reading him the biblical story of how Satan tried to tempt Jesus with visions of worldly success during forty days' fasting in the wilderness, Victor interrupted and asked, "Excuse me, Father, but what does the devil look like?"

Father John looked surprised at first, then contemplative. Finally, he smiled and said, "Interesting question, Victor. Give me a few days—I'll see what I can come up with."

Victor waited with much excitement to see what the priest might show him. He imagined an image of a horrific monster with great big twisted horns like a ram's and glowing red eyes that matched the flames that it snorted out of its nose and mouth like a dragon.

After three days, Father John called Victor over to the library. When he arrived, the priest said, "Ah, Victor, I found what you need." On the table was a book already open to a page showing a picture of a guardian angel helping a boy and girl cross an old, rickety wooden bridge in a dark forest. The angel wore flowing white robes and had fair skin and long, golden curls. She cupped the children protectively beneath a magnificent expanse of feathered wings, glowing with an emanant light. Her expression was tender. Father John pointed his thick forefinger at her and said, "There, my boy, is the answer to your question."

Victor glanced up at his mentor. "But I don't understand, Father. How can this be a picture of the devil? This is a picture of a beautiful angel helping children cross the bridge."

"Ah, but that is precisely what the devil would want you to think," Father John replied. "That he's an angel who is only trying to help you. How do you know this isn't Satan in disguise, leading the children toward their doom? Remember, my son, the devil started as the most beautiful of God's angels. His name was Lucifer, which means Bearer of Light. His light was more dazzling than any of Heaven's other angels, and he soared highest among them. Yet he fell to the deepest part of hell because he refused to accept God's will to honor man above the angels through his Son, Jesus

Christ. Since then, the devil has been waging war against mankind. Remember this, my son, and you won't go astray."

But somewhere along the way, Victor forgot and went astray. He sees it now—how he was blinded by all that glittered around the Madam. She was both angel and devil to him. Yet at the time, he saw only her luminous beauty, her regal style, and the bouts of tenderness and generosity that made her appear like an angel to many—including him. She discovered and adopted him just like she discovered and took Peachy under her wing.

She'd caught him in the dawn of his fame.

CHAPTER 10

After Mount Banahaw, Victor first settled in Tagaytay, a picturesque agricultural town overlooking Taal Lake. The lake was formed from a crater created by a volcanic eruption hundreds of years ago that gradually filled with freshwater. It surrounded and embraced Vulcan Point, a small, rocky volcano island that projected from the water's surface like a gaping mouth of the raging inferno underneath. More commonly known as Taal Volcano, it also cradled another crater lake at its navel, from which arose a slim trail of steam that served as a reminder it was alive—indeed, the most active, albeit lowest-height, volcano in the country. While it slept, the landscape was a temple to beauty, fertility, and tranquility, but when it awoke, it wreaked havoc upon the surrounding towns for hundreds of miles around.

Blessed with a temperate climate and rich volcanic soil, Tagaytay was ideal for growing the small but very sweet variety of pineapples and bananas it was known for, along with other fruits, such as coconuts, grapefruit, star apples, and jackfruit. Victor signed up with a local farm as a fruit and vegetable picker. Barely into his twenties, he looked a mere boy, yet was bursting with ancient knowledge. He lived and worked as the others did—close to the earth, high up on the emerald ridge that overlooked the silver-blue lake.

A fellow worker, Doroteo, had a makeshift bamboo and grass shack beside his family's nipa hut that he offered to Victor. The structure was skeletal. It didn't even have a proper door, just an old shell curtain that made soft tinkling music when one passed through it, or when the breezes made it dance. But it was perfect for Victor. He imagined himself a hermit in the wilderness, setting the stage for his life's work. There, he spent many happy, solitary evenings communing with his Twin Spirit under a moon that looked like a big, ripe guava—a pale yellow orb, lucent and ready for the picking. Up on those hills, it did seem as if one could simply reach out and grab the sweet, tangy fruit of the gods on whose skin was rightly tattooed the image of the crowned Queen of Heaven holding her Divine Infant Child. Victor took that to be a sign that the Blessed Mother herself was faithfully watching over him as she had on that fateful, stormy night that had brought him to Father John's chapel. It thus disheartened Victor to discover later on in America that the shadows on the face of the moon took on the shape of a mere rabbit. *An animal had replaced the Madonna and Child!* He would interpret this as another sign of the Divine's abandonment of him.

In Tagaytay, the Divine was with him and in him, and so it was there that Victor performed his first big miracle. One afternoon, while he and Doroteo were harvesting banana clusters, Victor heard what sounded like an animal shrieking and howling nearby. He ran to where he thought he'd heard the cries and found his friend writhing on the ground like an earthworm bisected by a mischievous child. Doroteo appeared to have accidentally hacked his arm with his bolo.

"Brother, help me!" Doroteo weakly cried.

Doroteo's hand remained attached by mere shreds of bone and skin. Victor quickly tore off his own shirt and wrapped it around his friend's mangled limb. He knelt down beside Doroteo and proceeded to call upon his Twin Spirit for guidance. He'd always wondered how he'd feel the first time he facilitated a solo miracle, and imagined himself quite nervous. He was pleasantly surprised to find himself completely calm, his soul in total communion with his Twin Spirit. He remembered what the *arbolario* had told him—to not be afraid if he wasn't sure what to do, to just go through the ritual and allow his Twin Spirit to move his hands for him. He took off the medallion he wore around his neck and laid it on Doroteo's prostrate body. With his eyes closed, he prayed, "Oh, beloved Santo Niño, you are the all-compassionate Healer. I offer my hands as a channel for your graces. Let your Light unite this broken body once again and your Life flow back to this limb. This I ask in the name of the Son, invoking the blessings of the Holy Spirit and the infinite compassion of the Father-Mother."

Almost instantly, a bubbling energy emanated from his gut and surged through his heart, then toward his arms, and down to his fingertips. He held Doroteo's arm and hand, wrapping both his own hands around the injured part. He then chanted the Latin words and trusted in their power, as he trusted in all that the *arbolario* had taught him on Mount Banahaw. He felt his own hand separate from his arm, giving him Doroteo's pain, and he would have fainted himself were it not for the spinning ball of fire in his gut that kept him upright and conscious. All through this, he kept his eyes closed. When he felt the energy subside, he fell exhausted to the earth alongside his friend.

He wasn't sure how long after that he heard the voices of other people. A woman asked, "Doroteo, Victor! What happened? Are you all right?"

When Victor opened his eyes, he saw Doroteo lying beside him, dazed and confused, as though having forgotten what had happened to him. Then, as if suddenly remembering, his friend registered panic, sat up, and peeled away Victor's bloodied shirt from his wrist. When his hand revealed itself attached to his arm, he cried out, *"Dios ko po!* My God—he has put it back! I had accidentally cut off my hand, but look! Victor has restored it! *Milagro!"* Doroteo held up his hand for everyone to see—unharmed and pristine as any healthy man's hand can be, save for the dried blood that still stained his skin. *"Maraming salamat,* Victor! Thank you! How can I ever repay you?"

"Don't thank me, my friend," Victor calmly replied. "Thank God, instead."

News of the miracle—the great *milagro,* people called it—soon spread around Tagaytay.

One early morning, not long after Doroteo's accident and miraculous recovery, an old man came asking for Victor. "Sincerest apologies for disturbing you, sir," he said to Victor, who noted his use of the deferential address.

"What can I do for you, *Tatay?"* Victor paid the customary respect to the older man by using the word for "father."

"Sir, my name is Pablo. I am caretaker for Villa Rodriguez. My master, Don Hidalgo, arrived yesterday. He's been up since last night with great pain in his legs and feet. Won't you please come, young master, to help him?"

Victor rode with Pablo toward the Rodriguez mansion in a highlands estate overlooking the lake. He had never seen a house so palatial. Pablo drove the car past tall, wrought-iron gates on a cobbled driveway that circled a garden with a stone fountain. The car stopped before tiled steps that led up to huge double wooden doors ornately carved with tropical birds and flowers.

The caretaker rang the bell. Soon, a plump middle-aged woman whom Victor assumed was the housekeeper peeked out of one of the doors. "Lucia," Pablo said, "this is Victor Mariano. He has come to help *Amo.*"

"Oh-hoh-hoh!" the woman gasped, covering her mouth. She threw the door open and quickly grasped Victor's hands, kissing them. By now, Victor had become accustomed to older people kissing his hand and bringing it to their fore-heads—an act of respect typically reserved for older people and persons of authority. "Please follow me, sir," she said, as she led him to another part of the house. Pablo followed.

"Don Hidalgo is in his library," Lucia said. "He was reading there after dinner last night before he called me to complain of the pain in his feet. They are so swollen, he could not even walk back to his bedroom. Pablo and I could not carry him to his bed because he is so heavy. So he has been there since last night. I did the best I could. Been soaking his feet in iced water. I hope that is all right, sir?" She glanced at Victor, who nodded.

The housekeeper's chattering faded into a buzz in Victor's ears as they entered the mansion. He was drawn to the many big and shiny things in the house, disappointed that they were walking too fast for him to properly see and ad-mire them all. Past the front doors, a huge, brilliant crystal chandelier greeted him from the high ceiling. Man-height oriental jars with gold-trimmed edges and jewel-colored scenes of Asian poets and aristocrats frolicking in sculpted gardens stood at the entry to the *sala*—the receiving parlor resplendent with gleaming glass and marble surfaces, ornately carved furniture, and jewel-hued fabrics. He saw the majestic view of Taal Lake and its volcano from the expansive glass windows and sliding doors that framed the home's back side. Even the house's smell was rich with the scents of flowers, wax-polished hardwood floors, cigars, and leather.

Lucia finally led Victor inside a darkened room whose curtains were drawn. It was lit only by the amber light of a glass-shaded lamp that sat on a gigantic carved wooden desk. As Victor's eyesight gradually adjusted to the dimness of the room, he saw walls lined with wooden shelves filled with leather-bound books. He'd later recall the scent of those books whenever he entered Professor Morrison's room at Casa del Sol.

Gilt-framed oil paintings featuring humble subjects were interspersed among Don Hidalgo's books, filling the room with smiling farmers bent over rice fields and smiling laundrywomen clad only in *tapises,* washing clothes in large *batyas* by a stony river bank—their young, naked children playfully splashing water at each other nearby—and fruit vendors smiling their toothless smiles, squatting on the ground behind large woven baskets filled with colorful harvests. Victor knew these people. He saw their faces among those he lived with—indeed always smiling, no matter how hard their lives were.

A wretched groan drew Victor's attention from the radiant artworks to a corner of the room. He spied someone seated there with his feet soaking in a tub. Victor asked Lucia and

Pedro to draw the curtains open to let the sunlight in. When he approached the person, he saw an obese man who looked to be in his seventies, a pathetic creature wrapped in a navy blue silk kimono.

As the drapes were opened, the man winced at the bright light, shielding his eyes with his hands. "*Santa Maria!*" Don Hidalgo cried. "Keep those curtains closed!"

"Forgive us, *Amo,*" Lucia said, addressing him as servants addressed their masters, "but this is the faith healer we were telling you about. Victor Mariano. He has come to cure your feet."

Don Hidalgo removed fat fingers from his eyes and, after straining to get a good look at his visitor, appeared taken aback. Victor knew that look—the one that told him he was not good enough, that because of the color of his skin and the strangeness of his appearance, he was suspect. Ignoring Don Hidalgo's reaction, he said, "Good morning, sir."

Perhaps it was sheer physical pain that prevented the old man from dwelling upon whatever prejudice he was pre-disposed to, for he then replied, "Can you help me? My gout has started again, and I can't walk or sleep. It's been very painful."

Victor knelt to inspect the man's feet and was shocked by how swollen they were. The man's big toes looked like bananas; his feet, lumpy coconuts. His ankles had completely disappeared into his legs. The chair on which Don Hidalgo sat turned out to be a recliner, so Victor asked Lucia and Pedro to help him push it into a horizontal position. The old man groaned as they did this. Victor then asked for two candles to be lit and held by each servant near the man's head and feet. When this was accomplished, he addressed his patient. "Don Hidalgo, do you believe in the all-merciful God, in His Holy Spirit of Love, and in His Son, the all-compassionate Healer?"

The old man mumbled, "Yeah, yeah. I believe in all that—now, let's get on with it."

Victor paused. "Don Hidalgo, I can't do this without you. Your sincere faith is necessary."

The rich man looked startled by Victor's admonishment. "It's just—it's so painful! I can't bear it any longer. I am sorry."

Victor continued, "Do you value your soul more than this passing mortal body?"

"Yes—yes, of course."

"Do you repent of your sins and vow not to commit them again?"

The old man met Victor's gaze and replied with a solemn, "Yes."

"Then be still and be grateful, Don Hidalgo, for God in His loving mercy will now heal you of what ails you."

Victor proceeded to recite the usual prayers to his Twin Spirit, synchronizing his body's vibrations with those of the suffering parts of the man's body like a metal detector that tracked where the treasure hid. He put his medallion on the man's feet, legs, and over the kidney. Retrieving the red and white stones from a jute sack he carried, he placed the sacred pebbles on the man's solar plexus and chanted the usual Latin incantation. He withdrew a small bottle of conse-crated coconut oil from the sack and massaged the ointment all over the man's feet, toes, and ankles. Soon, reddish and yellowish juices began to ooze out of the man's skin around the ailing parts, dripping into the tub below. The process might have been painful, yet Don Hidalgo seemed to feel no discomfort. Within minutes, his legs and feet returned to their normal size.

"*Susmaryosep!*" Lucia exclaimed. "Look at him, he's sleeping like a baby."

"Avoid feeding him sweets, salty foods, red meat, and shellfish—especially mussels and oysters," Victor advised her. "I tasted them as I worked his body. And alcohol—no more liquor."

"But those are all his favorites!" Lucia objected.

"It's his choice. God can only do so much. Man must do his part," Victor declared.

Lucia replied, "Yes, sir. Of course, sir, Mr. Mariano. Thank you. Don Hidalgo will reward you greatly for this."

"Tell him I wish for nothing else—except perhaps . . . to build a chapel dedicated to El Negro Santo Niño de Jesus." Victor hadn't planned this response, but the words came out of his mouth as if he had.

Subsequently, news of Victor's miraculous healing powers spread throughout the country. Reporters who had heard of the miracles in Tagaytay came and watched as the young healer performed his magic. They shot photos and filmed as Victor closed a girl's cleft palate; restored the polio-afflicted leg of a boy, allowing him to walk without the aid of a crutch; took out, with his bare hands, an infected appendix; and accomplished, with just his fingers burying themselves in skin and flesh, a bloodless caesarean operation that delivered an infant past its birth time who was stubbornly turned the wrong way in his mother's womb. The mother's stomach retained no ugly scar—just a faint pink line at the center.

AMAZING FAITH HEALER IN TAGAYTAY! Victor's accomplishments were in the headlines for months. People from all walks of life, from towns and provinces far and near, came to the lowly grass hut where Victor received them. He refused to move to better accommodations, although many had offered him homes built of sturdy concrete blocks with galvanized metal roofs.

His friends—fellow fruit and vegetable pickers—volunteered to work in shifts to form a security circle around Victor, keeping watch day and night so their local legend and treasure was not harmed in any way. They also saw this as an opportunity to set up fruit, food, and drink vending stalls along the roads leading to Victor's place. Doroteo took on the role of Victor's manager, acting as both receptionist and spokesman.

Victor didn't have to continue working as a farmhand to feed himself, for his neighbors and patients provided all he needed: rice, fruit, vegetables, eggs, fowl, and sometimes even the occasional modest monetary gifts. From the wealthy, Victor asked only for contributions to finish the chapel of the Black Santo Niño that Don Hidalgo had already started. The wealthy man had donated part of his estate overlooking the lake as a site for the chapel.

Don Hidalgo's many enterprises included timber. Through his lumber concessions, Don Hidalgo procured precious narra wood and commissioned a famous sculptor from Pampanga province to carve it into a two-foot statue of El Negro Santo Niño as a gift to Victor. Narra wood was especially valued not only because it was rare by then, found only in the fast-disappearing old-growth forests of the Philippine archipelago, but also because of its extraordinarily dense and fine texture that rendered it almost as hard as stone. The sculpture of the Child-God turned out magnificently, and Victor was immensely pleased by it. The statue's countenance was marked by a playful smile, his right hand poised in a gesture of blessing as he held the whole world steady on his left hand. Victor liked that the carver had left the wood unpainted and unstained except for a thin layer of beeswax rubbed over its surface to enhance its natural dark color and smooth texture. He loved and prized the narra statue of the Black Child Jesus more than anything he'd ever owned.

Victor especially liked the mythical symbolism associated with the narra wood. Philippine legend said the narra tree was a gift of the god Bathala to the first man and woman who had emerged from a giant bamboo trunk after it was struck and split by lightning. Although born from the pliant bamboo, the first couple was instructed by Bathala to build their home from solid narra. This story left a great impression upon Victor as a schoolboy, mainly because it was so different from the Judeo-Christian story he'd learned in religion class. In the biblical story, God created Eve, the first woman, from one of the ribs God plucked out of Adam, the first man. The woman eventually caused man's downfall and was the source of original sin. Victor preferred the woman in the Philippine creation story, because she was neither man's inferior nor man's downfall. She was, rather, man's equal half: as strong, beautiful, and virtuous as her male partner. *The mother I never had, the woman I could never be.*

CHAPTER 11

Victor perched on the top step of the bamboo stoop of his Tagaytay hut. The heat of the noonday sun bore down upon him. He could feel his energy waning. He had already spent the whole morning curing dozens of the afflicted people who'd been lining up in front of his dwelling since dawn.

A cloud of dust announced the approach of a convoy of vehicles. Everyone, including Victor, watched as a sleek black limousine led and guarded by a pair of police motorcycles and two white sedans pulled up on the dirt road leading to his shack. The limousine's dark-tinted windows made it impossible to see its passenger.

About ten men emerged from the cars, handguns dangling from holsters under their armpits and hips. Though they wore no uniforms, there was no mistaking who they were. They stood by the vehicles, surveying the crowd. One approached Victor's hut and demanded with an air of authority, "Who among you is Victor Mariano?"

Doroteo came forward and replied with equal authority, "Who wants to know?"

"A very important person."

"What important person? We are all important in God's eyes."

"Shut up!" the man snapped. "If you know what's good for you. Where's this Victor Mariano?"

"Here he is. I am he," Victor calmly answered. "Tell your lady I will be with her in a moment."

Doroteo looked at Victor with surprise, and as the latter walked down the steps, Doroteo blocked his path and whispered, "Victor, are you sure about this?"

"Don't worry, my friend, it's all right."

Victor followed the man until they reached the limousine. The man opened the passenger door for him. The hum of the car engine sounded like the steady breathing of a vigilant watchdog. Inside the dark, air-conditioned vehicle, Victor came face to face with the most beautiful woman he had ever seen. He had been expecting her. He had seen her in a dream the night before—one of the glimpses of the future that the spirit world sometimes granted him.

"What can I do for you, madam?"

"Ah, Mr. Mariano, thank you for meeting me." She spoke with the voice of a loving mother.

"There is no choice when destiny calls."

"Then we are of like mind, for I, too, believe in destiny. Please come in and sit with me."

"Thank you, madam." Victor sat facing the woman.

"I have heard a lot about you, especially from my friend Don Hidalgo. And if all is true of what I've heard, you may be the one my husband and I need to help our poor, sick countrymen."

"How is that, madam?"

"Victor . . . may I call you that? I feel you are already a son to me."

He nodded.

"Victor, as you know, many of our countrymen cannot

afford to pay doctors to treat their many maladies. And even when I give them free clinics, doctors can only do so much. The medical sciences have their limitations. But I know the power of faith. Our people need someone who can appeal to God, someone they can believe in, someone who will tell them God is on our . . . I mean, *their* side."

"But madam, please understand. My services are not for hire. Nor am I empowered to use my gift to glorify any human—not even myself. I have nothing to do with politics."

"No one is hiring you, Victor. You are your own boss in this matter. And neither will you have to get into politics—in fact, we prefer you stay out of it. Just be yourself—a healer! I only want to help you by providing you with a bigger, more efficient setup to help everyone who needs you. This would glorify no one except God Himself."

Victor looked into her eyes, for instinct told him to remain skeptical. She returned his gaze before she pointed outside, where, even in that temperate part of the country, the sun's heat could be seen in dusty waves above the earth—a sharp contrast to the almost freezing temperature of the car's soft-leathered interior.

"Look," she said. "Look at all those poor, sick people out there—trekking these narrow dirt roads to reach you. Can you imagine what will happen a month from now when the typhoon season begins—or even a week from now? When more will hear of the great healer of Tagaytay? They will come in droves—in numbers much more than this small town can hold. Already you have outgrown this place. There are no public bathrooms around here. These pilgrims simply do their thing behind the bushes. What do you think that will do? Spread more diseases—that's what! Of course, if you're as good as they say you are, you will cure all of them, but it'll be a vicious cycle. It'll be like swatting flies—no matter how many you get, many more will come from nowhere. Whether you like it or not, your undertaking here already poses a threat to public health and safety. The Minister of Public Health is already all over us on this. But I told him to give me a chance to talk to you. I want to provide you with the facilities you need to better service our people and safeguard public health."

There was no arguing with her logic. He could already tell she was a lot smarter than people thought. "What then do you propose, madam?"

"I want to sponsor you. I want to bring you to Manila and give you a home there—and a clinic in the palace where you will be free to dispense God's healing to mankind. For the poor, your services will be free. For the rich, there will be an opportunity to donate to a worthy cause. I will bring them to you. I will be your *padrona*. In return, I ask for one thing."

"And what is that, madam?"

"That you tell them the truth: that my husband and I are not the evil people our enemies say we are. I want to prove them all wrong—to show that I care. That my husband cares. By bringing you to them, they will know this. Many already believe you are heaven-sent."

Victor remained silent, contemplating the Madam's words.

"Could you do that, Victor? Could you please do this for me? It is only a little thing to ask for the greater good of our people. Don't you think?"

Victor didn't know what to say. He had a nagging feeling there was more to this than he was hearing, but he couldn't find fault with the Madam's statements. "Please give me some time to reflect and pray over this, madam," was all he could think of to say.

"Of course, *hijo.* How much time would you need?"

"Three days."

"Good. I shall send someone for your answer after that. In the meantime, please accept my gift to you and these people."

As if on cue, a white van with a gold-painted sign, CAFÉ LE PARIS CATERING, pulled up behind them. Victor then saw how the people quickly gathered around the van. The Madam stepped out of the car, gesturing to Victor to follow her.

With the usual pomp and flair for which she was known, she announced to the perplexed multitude, "My dear people of God, in humble thanksgiving for all the miraculous cures the Good Lord has generously bestowed upon us today through the divine healing hands of our blessed brother, Victor Mariano, your beloved president and I have come to help lighten your load by bringing you nourishment for your bodies as your hungry souls fully partake of the abundant spiritual food here. Thanks be to God! Alleluia! Alleluia! *Mabuhay* to all of you!" The armed goons swiftly turned from stern soldiers to friendly distributors of the boxed lunches before the applauding crowd.

By then, Victor's answer was a foregone conclusion. He quickly learned that the Madam never accepted "no" for an answer. She sent a limousine and an army colonel, no less, to fetch him three days later.

CHAPTER 12

The road to perdition, Victor discovered, wasn't a speedy, slippery slope of self-destruction. It was a slow, imperceptible descent that, on the contrary, felt like ascent.

For him, it started with losing Doroteo. No, Victor couldn't take his friend, Colonel Ramirez said when he came to fetch Victor. The Madam only wanted him. Victor and Doroteo exchanged puzzled glances. Victor was about to protest when Doroteo said, "Don't worry, Victor. I will visit you later." Doroteo glanced at the colonel before he whispered to Victor, "To make sure you're okay."

When they reached Manila, the colonel brought Victor to a luxuriously furnished townhouse in Mabini. The Madam's secretary greeted him there and showed him to a sumptuous dinner awaiting him, catered again by Café le Paris. At first, Victor thought it was someone else's home and he was to be a guest there for the night. But the secretary said, "Welcome home, Mr. Mariano. This is your home now—a gift from the Madam. You'll find all you need here, but if there's anything else you want, please don't hesitate to call—here's my number. Madam says to take good care of you. She expects you first thing in the morning in the palace. I'll send a car to pick you up at seven."

Looking back on those first days in the city, when every-thing was suddenly handed to him on a big, shining silver platter, Victor could acknowledge that he should have seen disaster coming. But he'd accepted it all too easily. Some part of his mind rationalized it, seduced by the notion that the world owed it to him, that this was his reward for the pain of his childhood, for the rejection he suffered from his own mother, and for the insults, humiliations, and hatred he'd withstood—all because of the fateful accident of the color of his skin and the nature in which he was made.

Madam had reserved a separate building at the palace grounds as the site for her new project, Alay ng Puso, or "Heart Offering." It consisted of a free clinic for the masses whose crowning glory was Victor Mariano, the amazing faith healer from Tagaytay—now the fast-rising star among the Madam's protégés. She allowed Victor the freedom and power to supervise the outfitting of the facilities with a re-ceiving room, diagnostic room, and operating room. Victor placed the operating room adjacent to a chapel dedicated to the Black Santo Niño so that when an operation was in progress, a set of sliding doors could be opened to reveal the marvelous altar of the child deity and thereby make divine power more accessible for the procedure's success.

One freedom Victor learned he did not have was in the se-lection of his assistants. He asked for Doroteo, but Madam's secretary told him his friend couldn't be found. Victor had to settle for a staff member who, the secretary assured him, could be fully trusted. But Victor continued to inquire about his friend until Colonel Ramirez finally told him that Doro-teo was gone, killed on some mountain in Laguna province where he had allegedly led a subversive cell of Communist guerrillas responsible for the deaths of several soldiers.

It never occurred to Victor to question the report, although he was surprised to learn Doroteo was capable of such acts. He could only weep and pray for his friend. Madam expressed her fullest sympathies to Victor. She was the epitome of compassion, even sponsoring a requiem Mass for Doroteo at the Santo Niño chapel in petition for the poor misguided soul whom she said had fallen prey to the sorry brainwashing of the Communists.

"It is a tragedy that people like Doroteo mistake our generosity as a manipulation of the masses," she said. "But my husband and I forgive them. They don't know any better, these poor, uneducated people. They fail to see the light, unlike our blessed brother here, Victor Mariano." Something in Victor rebelled against the way Madam characterized Doroteo, but yet again, he couldn't find fault in her logic. He felt as if he was being swept away by a powerful tide he couldn't fight.

He'd met Peachy by then, who casually suggested he simply go with the Madam's flow, which he did. The trouble was, he went with the Madam's flow for far too long—much longer than even Peachy did.

At Alay ng Puso, multitudes of the poor, sick, and weary came to Victor in endless lines outside the walls of Malacañang, waiting to receive the miracles of the Madam's compassion. The puppet press fully covered the spectacle, recording each miracle for all to witness and reporting that this indeed was a blessed administration, ordained to rule by God. The free clinics were conducted every Monday, Wednesday, and Friday. Saturdays were reserved for a select few—the closed circle of Marcos friends and cronies. They showed their gratitude through their unstinting donations to the El Negro Santo Niño de Jesus Foundation, an organization established by the Madam as a fund-raising vehicle to support her various charitable projects.

Victor was grateful to be part of a system that brought relief to many suffering people. As far as he cared to see, the Madam was nothing if not generous, sincere in her intentions, and faithful to her commitment both to the people and him. She had opened a bank account for him, into which her secretary deposited regular monthly funds for his maintenance—an allowance generous enough to sustain a prince's life.

He accepted it all without question.

CHAPTER 13

Hearing a door open behind him while mopping the second-floor balcony hallway, Victor pauses to turn and see who it is.

"Hello, Tita Vee! How's it goin'?"

It's Eric, the hunk of a physical therapist who comes in to soothe old bones and sore muscles. As usual, he is wearing a plain white cotton crewneck shirt over short—*very short*—running shorts. Both garments showcase the contours of the young man's tall, hard, muscular frame. The shirt highlights his champion pecs and abs, and the sleeves, which he rolls high on his arms, reveal more of the lad's bulging muscles. And his legs—*oh, his long, chiseled legs!*—they are the best. Victor is almost afraid to look at him, but he looks anyway. He privately calls him his "Adonis." Like a Greek god, Eric has piercing yet playful eyes; dark, shiny, wavy hair tucked behind perfectly shaped ears; and a strong, angular jaw and cheekbones. His tanned complexion hints of many days spent surfing at Malibu beach, the nearby playground of Hollywood celebrities.

Victor stammers when he responds to Eric's greeting. "Oh! Hi, Eric. You're . . . early today."

The young man walks past Victor. "Yeah. Mr. Pinkard wanted a morning massage—had a bad time during the seniors' walk yesterday."

Just then, an old woman steps out of a room straight into Eric's path, colliding with him. Her handbag falls to the floor, scattering its contents. Fortunately, Eric is able to catch and hold her steady. "Whoa, sweetheart! Are you all right? I'm so sorry."

She nods, straightening her eyeglasses, appearing momentarily disoriented. Eric squats to retrieve the contents of her bag for her. The position pulls the young man's shorts low enough to allow Victor a magnificent view of the pair of dimples that crown the creamy swell of his buttocks.

"Here you are, ma'am. All gathered and accounted for." Eric is all smiles and charm as he hands the handbag to the old woman, who smiles back.

"Oh. Thank you, young man." Her flushed face and admiring expression betray her own enchantment with the handsome creature.

"Well, I'm off. Have a great day, folks!" Eric waves to them and glides down the hallway toward the stairs.

"Beautiful boy, isn't he?" a scratchy, baritone voice says behind Victor. Victor turns to see the voice's owner, a bare-chested, sixty-something man leaning on the doorframe of his room, clad only in a white towel tucked under his huge belly. The sight of Mr. Pinkard's wide, hairy, sagging chest above his equally hairy overhanging stomach ruins Victor's pleasant visions of Adonis. Victor notes how the old man watches Eric's receding figure with an unmistakably lascivious smile, before puffing on a cigarette.

"Wouldn't you just like to sample those delicious dumplings yourself?" Mr. Pinkard sighs.

With a gasp, the old woman quickly turns to walk toward the elevator, mumbling as she passes by Mr. Pinkard, "Pervert!"

Victor is livid. "Mr. Pinkard!" he exclaims. "You know the rules—no smoking in the common areas! And—full clothing with shoes, please! And—no scandalizing and riling up the residents!"

Mr. Pinkard guffaws as Victor forcibly pushes him inside his room, pulling the door shut.

It occurs to Victor that Mr. Pinkard might be gay. While Victor feels no guilt for his own admiration of men like Eric, the thought of an obnoxious person like Mr. Pinkard imposing himself on his young Adonis nauseates him. He knows that Mr. Pinkard is among the more affluent residents of the facility—and one of the youngest too. But for all of Mr. Pinkard's money, Victor wonders why the SOB doesn't just opt for home care if he truly needs assisted living. He wants to punch Mr. Pinkard in the face. *Too late.*

Victor finds himself sweating. *Punyemas! What is happening to me?* The fury crawls up his neck, travels to his head, and heart palpitations follow. The last few days have been unusually difficult, the incident with Mrs. Stanley only aggravating matters. If he were a woman, he might dismiss the recent hot flashes, temper snaps, and the amorphous sense of anxiety he's been experiencing as menopausal symptoms. After all, he is at the right age for it. But he is not a woman— a normal woman, that is. Maybe that's part of his anger. *To be half woman, half man!* Victor wants to scream.

CHAPTER 14

For many years, Victor only had the vaguest notion of his sexuality. He took for granted that the spiritual world he lived in left him with no desire for the pleasures of the flesh. After all, his two mentors, the *arbolario* and Father John, were celibates.

Moreover, what he had witnessed at the Brown Fox gave him an acute distaste for sex. His *Ninang* Jo-Ann had often assigned him the unpleasant tasks of being the night watch boy for the entry hall to the bedrooms and changing the sheets in the morning. He detested the animal sounds people made in those rooms—especially his mother's. He despised the crusty brown stains and fishy scent of sweat and other bodily fluids that clung to the sheets, remaining there long after several washings. He knew, because he often had to wash the sheets himself.

Most of all, the violations to his body that he had suffered at Manila City Jail didn't offer him any positive concept of sexuality. They taught him that men were not desirable creatures, only beings to be feared, hated, respected, or pitied, depending on the type of men they were. They were never objects of passion and desire.

Until he met Richard Reyes.

It started as a magical night. Peachy had concluded yet another well-received fashion show. Victor had been enraptured by the parade of swaying silks, chiffons, and hand-painted satin *ternos* and *sayas* in pastel colors worn by the female models, as well as the somber procession of elegant linens and piña cloths embroidered and tailored in the latest *Barong Tagalog* styles modeled by the men. One particular model stood out from the rest.

"Who's the new guy?" Victor asked Peachy as they both admired the tall, slim, movie star look-alike who strutted and swaggered on the catwalk.

"His name is Richard Reyes. Why? You interested?"

Victor felt disconcerted. It hadn't yet occurred to him that what he felt was desire. "What? Me? Of course not—just curious."

"Yeah, right." Peachy giggled, poking Victor in the ribs.

The show was followed by a reception marked by seemingly endless cocktails, hors d'oeuvres, and an extravagant display of sparkling gems not only on turkey throats and fat fingers but also on the gorgeous bodies of beauty queens and movie stars. When the party finally ended in the early morning hours, Peachy invited Victor to come home with him. Considering the time, Victor agreed. When he entered the car that would take them to Peachy's penthouse, he was surprised to find Peachy's boyfriend and Richard Reyes already seated inside. Victor's heart jumped at the sight of the beautiful man.

"What's going on?" Victor whispered to his friend.

"Just helping to satisfy your curiosity," Peachy whispered back.

More drinks and some pot-smoking followed when they arrived at Peachy's place. After a while, Peachy and his boyfriend disappeared into a bedroom, and Victor was left alone with Richard on the living room couch, both of them slouched against the oversized cushions. All the wine, liquor, and weed had become a fuzz ball in Victor's brain. He felt light as air. Devoid of inhibition.

Victor reached out to brush part of Richard's silky bangs out of his eyes. "You are so beautiful."

"You think so?" Richard glanced sideways at Victor, his lips curled into a naughty smile above the rim of a wine goblet.

"Yes. I think so."

"Is there anything wrong, then?"

"What do you mean?" Victor laughed nervously.

"I mean, don't you want me?" Richard murmured. "You've not made a move on me. I almost feel insulted."

"Insulted? No, don't be! Why, I . . . never thought . . . never dreamed to . . ."

"What—to want me or to have me? Victor, baby, you know you want me. To have me, all you need is to claim me." The young man rested his glass on the coffee table, kissed Victor passionately on the mouth, knelt on the floor, and unzipped Victor's pants—an action Victor instinctively resisted, albeit inadequately.

His body responded and opened up to Richard's lovemaking. A sizzling current of delight arced and simmered into a warm haze of pure pleasure inside Victor until all concept of who he was faded in the steamy enchantment of the moment.

Until the scream. Richard's scream. The would-be lover had discovered Victor's secret. The look on the young man's face was one of pure disgust.

"*Pweh!*" He spat in Victor's face. "Who are you? *What* are *you?*" He grabbed Victor by the collar and hit him. He was about to strike again when a half-naked Peachy ran out of the bedroom, yelling, "Stop! Stop! What is going on?"

"Your friend here—he's a weirdo! I don't do weirdoes." Richard released Victor and extended his hand to Peachy. "Give us our money now—we wanna split. Hey, Dave! Time to go, man!"

Peachy went back to the bedroom and returned with a thick envelope that he handed to Richard. The latter turned to his buddy, who was only then coming out of the bedroom. "C'mon, Dave—let's leave these freaks to their freakin' selves!" He spat on the floor on the way out. The door banged shut behind them.

At first, Victor struggled to comprehend what had happened. He understood Richard had gotten upset when he'd discovered Victor was not all he appeared to be. What Victor didn't immediately grasp was the matter about the money— until he remembered Peachy's words. *Just helping to satisfy your curiosity.*

Peachy was examining his face. "Oh, dear, oh dear, oh dear! I'm so sorry about that, *chica*!" He pulled a couple of tissues from the box on the coffee table and pressed them to Victor's nose, which was dripping blood. "Hang on—I'm gonna get you some ice for that shiner."

"Don't bother." Victor turned to look at Peachy.

His eyes must have reflected all the bitterness he felt, because Peachy countered with, "What are you looking at me like that for? You enjoyed yourself while it lasted, didn't you?" It was the first time Peachy had raised his voice at him.

Memories of his mother's many lovers rushed into Victor's head. He yelled back, "Of course it matters. I don't buy love!"

"You didn't. I did . . . for you!" Peachy snapped back. "And you're a fool if you think people like us can get *any* loving for free, let alone real love."

Victor rushed to go out the door, but Peachy blocked him. "Look, Victor. I'm sorry. I only had good intentions. You know I care for you, *chica*. Don't leave like this."

"I don't deserve cheapness."

Peachy's expression shifted again. He stepped aside, pointing to the door. "Go on, then. Go! Don't you think it's a little late worrying about how cheap you've become? Just in case you still don't know, Victor, we're both nothing but whores in Madam's kingdom."

The two friends eventually reconciled, but their friendship wasn't the same. A few months later, Peachy announced he was leaving for America. Peachy constantly reassured Victor their quarrel wasn't the cause of his departure, but Victor was never fully convinced. He blamed himself.

CHAPTER 15

Victor heads back to the dining pavilion, where he and other staff members had earlier started decorating a section for Mrs. Langley's great-granddaughter's birthday party the next day. The large room is shaped like a donut around a spherical garden with an old oak tree at the center. The building has floor-to-ceiling glass windows to maximize views of the lovely courtyard. The pavilion's layout allows for certain portions of the dining room to be partitioned, like pieces of a sliced pie, for private resident functions. Several French doors open onto the garden, allowing each party to have its own access.

In the past two weeks, Victor avoided dwelling on the vexatious Mrs. Stanley by focusing on assisting the angelic Mrs. Langley with preparations for Chrissie's birthday party. He helped plan and coordinate the party menu with the kitchen, recruited the help of a couple other staff members, and shopped for the decor, craft, and game materials they'd need. Victor is inspecting the pink and white garlands of twisted crepe paper strips already strung across parts of the wall and ceiling when he sees the old lady approaching, carrying something. "Well, what do you think, Mrs. Langley?"

"Why it's wonderful—simply wonderful, Tita Vee! Thank

you! By the way, this arrived from the printer—could you please help me hang this, too?

"No problem! I'd planned on it." Victor positions the step-ladder he earlier procured from storage, climbs it, and hangs the HAPPY BIRTHDAY, CHRISSIE! banner on the wall above where they plan to put the buffet table.

Mrs. Langley claps her hands delightedly. "That's beautiful, Tita Vee! Thank you!"

"You are very welcome, sweetie! I'll also make sure to hang the piñata and tie the balloons to the chairs as soon as they're delivered tomorrow."

Just then, Brenda comes running toward them. "Tita Vee! Tita Vee!"

"What is it, Brenda, dahling? I didn't expect you today."

Brenda is not her usual cheerful self. Her eyes dart about anxiously. "Mrs. Fernandez asked me to come in to cover for her. She left early for a weekend trip." Then, lowering her voice, she says, "Tita Vee, I need to talk to you."

"Sure," Victor replies. "Would you excuse us, Mrs. Langley?"

"Of course, hon. Thanks for your help."

As Victor steps down the ladder, Brenda grabs his elbow and steers him outside in the courtyard.

"What's going on?" Victor asks.

"Tita Vee, you haven't had a vacation in a long while, have you?"

"No. Why?"

"Well, now is a good time to take one."

"What do you mean?"

"You don't understand. You need to get lost—now!" Brenda says this under her breath, both her hands now grasping Victor's arms.

"But I can't—not right away. What about Mrs. Langley's

party? I promised to help. Besides, why do I have to get lost? I'm not sure I like the sound of that."

"I need to get back. I only wanted to warn you."

"Warn me about what?" Victor is beginning to feel alarmed.

"There were a couple of men who arrived just as I assumed my post. They asked whether we had a Victor Mariano among the staff."

"But who were they?" Victor frowns.

"Their IDs said they were INS."

"I-N what?"

"Immigration," Brenda says grimly, lowering her voice.

"Oh, dear."

"Tita Vee, there is a problem, isn't there?"

"I'm afraid so." His tourist visa had expired six months after his entry in the United States—five years ago. "But what did you say to them?"

"I had a feeling they meant trouble for you. So I said I didn't know, that I wasn't familiar with everyone yet. Since I'm fairly new and mainly assigned to the evening shift. Except today. Well, I do know you as Tita Vee, don't I?" Brenda growls, "I bet it's someone here who has squealed on you."

"But why? And who could it be?"

"Tita Vee, you've gotta get out of here before they see you. They asked if I minded if they looked around. I said I did—and didn't they need a warrant or something to check inside the premises? Good thing I picked up some lines from a few crime shows."

"And who says television can't be educational, huh?" Victor chuckles.

"Shh! Tita Vee, be serious now. This is far from over. They demanded to talk with the manager. I told them that it's too bad because Mrs. Fernandez had left for the weekend already. They said they'll return Monday. So you only have two days to disappear."

"But I can't possibly abandon Mrs. Langley now!"

"Victor, your situation is more urgent than Mrs. Langley's."

"I know . . . but . . . Thank you, Brenda. I don't know how I can repay you for this."

"Don't mention it. Do you know where you could go? Who can you run to?"

"I'm not sure." He thinks of calling Candace, who moved to San Francisco, and with whom he corresponded every Christmas. He worries their connection isn't substantial enough to support such imposition.

"Well, let me know if you need my help. Maybe you can room in with me for a while if you've nowhere else."

"I hate to impose on you, Brenda."

"You're not imposing at all, believe me. Just let me know. In the meantime, take care. Try to keep to your room if you can, okay? Don't be loitering around. They could return anytime! Don't even go out."

Just then, they hear one of the swing-out windows closing in a room above them. When they both look up, they catch the smiling, evil face of Mrs. Stanley fading into the shadows. They've forgotten how sounds from the garden tend to echo toward the rooms above. And that the hag has a good set of hearing aids.

Victor and Brenda exchange worried glances.

"Oh. My. God," Brenda says.

It's past midnight, but Victor can't sleep. Lying in the shadows, he observes the pale moonlight streaming in eerie rays through the partially open vertical blinds of his window. He hears the wheezing wind as it glides over the hills and valleys. Giving up on sleep, he turns on the bedside lamp and reaches for volume five of *Les Misérables.* He's been reading it since Mrs. Fernandez handed it to him, and when Professor Morrison returned from the hospital a week ago, he was kind enough to allow him to retain the book outside their reading hours. Victor has been devouring it, reading during any free time he's found—day and night, often into dawn. Sleep hasn't been a regular visitor lately.

As Victor turns to the last page, he realizes he's sweating. He feels the white heat that's been rising from his core slowly suffocating him. The novel's ending distresses him. It ended well for Jean Valjean, all right, but Javert's tragedy weighs him down. He's not sure whether he still identifies with Jean Valjean, or whether Javert is now a more accurate reflection of his state of mind and soul. He feels the hopelessness and despair that led Javert to suicide. But everything he's learned makes him averse to this. Yet how to escape the futility of one's life? *Who am I? Who do I choose to be?*

The incidents with Mrs. Stanley have awoken a demon in him, inciting tortuous memories of his mother. *How could such a mother have done what she did to her own child? Even animals sacrifice their lives to protect their young!* The hatred he'd held off feeling for Lorie all those years in the Philippines is now rushing to the surface, like Taal Volcano about to erupt. He'd refused to acknowledge it when he still had the gift, believing that his healing powers required him to be uncorrupted by dark thoughts and feelings as this. Now that the gift is gone, the demon of his soul has strengthened its hold over him. But how can he expel something he can't touch? How can he release his anger at someone long dead?

He draws the blinds to one side and slides the window open. A soft breeze cools his skin and rustles through the blinds. The sound reminds Victor of serene nights in his Tagaytay hut many years ago, when the pleasant tinkling of his shell curtain accompanied the symphonic singing of frogs, crickets, and lizards, and the occasional hooting owl. That was the last time he'd felt as perfectly whole as any human being could be—united and at peace with God, man, and earth.

Victor peers into the moonlit valley outside his window. The rugged play of light and shadow upon the crinkled landscape and the distant howling of a coyote fill him with foreboding. Leaves and branches quiver in the Santa Ana winds that blow across the Mexican desert into Southern California at this time of the year. Some locals call these winds El Diablo, a name that evokes the hell inherent in the constant threat of wildfires that can ignite and spread out of nowhere among the dry, brittle foliage. Some also believe it is the name of the impish spirit that rides the hot winds to haunt the souls of living men with the ghosts of their shame.

Just then, a gust of wind invades Victor's room, and his closet door swings open. The silvery light draws forth the shadowy shapes from their prison, and two figures reveal themselves from the darkness within. They are El Negro Santo Niño de Jesus and Nuestra Señora del Santo Rosario. Child deity and Goddess Mother stand side by side on a shelf, accusing him with their beady glass eyes. El Diablo could not have brought Victor any more haunting, taunting ghosts than these.

CHAPTER 16

It's Saturday afternoon, time for Chrissie's birthday party at Casa del Sol. Victor has decided to stick around, at least for this occasion. He didn't have the heart to abandon Mrs. Langley.

Tomorrow, he's leaving for San Francisco, where he hopes to stay with Candace until the situation with INS cools down. Brenda promised to help him procure an emergency work leave, but he fears this could be the end of his Casa del Sol days. He's on the TNT track now, the inescapable fate of the undocumented immigrant. He's going to miss Professor Morrison, Brenda, and Mrs. Langley for sure, but he couldn't say proper farewells without risking unwanted attention. Despite the challenging work, Casa Del Sol has been his home these last few years. To have to leave without saying good-bye to his friends feels like losing a limb and pretending nothing's happened—until the inevitable crippling reminders make it impossible.

After finishing tying the strings of the pink and white balloons to the chairs, Victor takes in the panorama of sugar and spice around him: the little pink and white carnation bouquet centerpieces, the clear pitchers of iced pink lemonade, the pink frosted birthday cake decorated with seven fuchsia sugar rosebuds, seven white candles, and the greeting, HAPPY 7TH BIRTHDAY, CHRISSIE! LOVE FROM GRANNY BLES.

The cake sits on the buffet table, surrounded by pink and white napkins, pink and white paper plates, and pink and white forks. Victor laments the macaroni-and-beef casserole and chicken salad sandwiches couldn't come in shades of pink and white, but he smiles nonetheless. It's a picture-perfect setting for a little girl who has so far proven to be more spice than sugar.

The guests start to arrive, greeted with utmost charm by Mrs. Langley. "Welcome, welcome, friends!"

"Oh, how lovely, Blesilda! Pink and white—how very charming and feminine."

"Why, thank you, Charlotte."

"Ugh! I feel itchy just looking at all this girly stuff, Bles. Anything for us old boys here?"

"Oh, don't be silly, Max! The party's not for you, after all. Now be a gentleman and find a seat—and no whining, please!"

"Blesilda, may I have one of the centerpieces when it's all over?"

"Why, of course Lilia—but just one, dear, all right?"

Mrs. Langley has invited various residents to attend—members of her bridge circle and her book club, fellow Episcopalians who go to Sunday services with her, and her ten a.m. Golden Yoga classmates. Victor wonders how seven-year-old Chrissie will feel about having people ten times her age as guests. But when the princess-brat finally arrives with her already exhausted-looking parents, she appears no less than a proud monarch descending upon her subjects. She's radiant in a pink-and-white ruffled organza dress cinched with a slim belt made of fuchsia silk roses. Victor supposes the opportunity to show off her new attire was enough of an incentive for the girl to come—that and the many gifts she was promised that day.

Mrs. Langley plays the doting great-grandma. "Oh, my little princess! Look at you, you're a refreshing sight for old eyes. Now, turn around and let's see that darling outfit. I declare—that's the most gorgeous dress on the prettiest girl in the whole wide world!"

"Thanks, Granny Bles," Chrissie replies, smiling and swirling to display how the full skirt of her dress expands like the petals of a blossom. Then with a serious expression, the girl asks, "Granny, where are my gifts? You promised!"

"Not yet, sweetie—after you blow out the candles on your cake later, all right? Then you may have them."

"Oh, okay." Chrissie pouts.

After all the guests arrive, Victor helps to serve the food. The macaroni casserole and chicken sandwiches, while not in pink and white, are delicious and kind to dentures.

Soon enough, Chrissie ends up getting her way, raiding the gift table before the cake has been served. She loses interest in each gift almost as soon as she tears off its wrapping. There are a few too many knitted pink mittens and scarves for the California girl, and she has received multiple identical Cinderella Barbie dolls in pink and white ball gowns.

It's time for the piñata, which hangs from one of the low-lying branches of the oak tree. Mrs. Langley invites everyone to go outside. "After all, one is never too old for candy," she says, to the delight of her guests.

Victor catches a whiff of wood smoke in the air and remembers hearing a news report about wildfires burning in

Simi Valley. The report said the fires are not of immediate concern for people in surrounding areas. Victor is surprised at the intensity of the smell.

The birthday celebrant gets to have the first try at hitting the hanging donkey. Her dad carries her on his shoulders to reach it. After missing quite a few times and failing to put a substantial dent in the mascot, she crosses defiant arms across her chest and stomps away from the crowd.

"Leave her alone!" her father yells to his wife and Mrs. Langley, who are about to go after the little rebel. "Both of you are spoiling her. She's got to learn it's not all about her."

Victor notes how the look in Chrissie's dad's eyes equals the defiance in his daughter's. *At least there's one person in the family who can stand up to the kid.*

The donkey-bashing game continues until old Max finally releases the candies, which rain down on the guests. Arthritic backs and creaky knees notwithstanding, everyone scrambles for the sweet treats lying on the ground. The old people proving they're still adept at this kind of physical competition amuse Victor. *Just like little children, only in old bodies!* As he watches the scramble, he feels bits of dust in his eye and notices ash particles come in with the breeze. *Must be strong winds to carry it this far.*

A few minutes later, he looks up from the neat circle of folding chairs he's finished setting up for the musical chairs game and catches two men looking out at the party scene from the dining room. He's never seen them before. Victor remembers what Brenda said about the INS agents. Perhaps it's their too-neat hairstyles, their khaki Dockers, their rigid stance, and their unshed sunglasses that give them away.

Both sets of sunglasses turn in unison to the old woman beside them. It's none other than Mrs. Stanley, who appears to be telling them something and is now pointing to Victor. The men exchange glances, nod, and begin to move toward where he is in the garden.

Uh-oh. Victor hurries toward a door that leads inside another portion of the dining area. Just before he reaches it, a hand grabs his arm. Turning around, he sees it is Mrs. Langley's. *Whew.*

"Tita Vee, have you seen Chrissie?"

The men are heading toward him from the opposite side of the garden.

"Don't worry, Mrs. Langley. I'll look for her," he says, slipping indoors.

"Thanks, Tita Vee. I'd like to serve the cake next. Do please get her in time . . ." Mrs. Langley's reply fades as the door closes on her. Victor swiftly crosses the dining room and heads to the main hallway that will take him around to his room. He has no intention of searching for Chrissie. *Sorry, Mrs. Langley, but I've gotta go.*

Perhaps retreating to his room is not the best move at this time. Maybe the men already know where his room is. He makes his way up the stairway to the second floor instead. When he reaches the landing, he sprints toward the storage room, stopping to make sure no one sees him. He unlocks the door, enters and locks himself in, intending to hide there until it's safe to reappear.

About half an hour later, Victor is sitting awkwardly on a box of toilet paper when he hears a series of shrieks coming from the hallway. They are loud enough to make him curious, so he peeks out the door. A few residents are also peeking out of their doors, frowning and asking each other what's going on. Then the shouting starts.

"So it's you! Ha! You rotten brat! Oh no! What have you done? Oh my God, what have you done?"

Victor comes out of hiding, compelled by the ferocity of the screams, instinctively following where they lead.

"All broken! Look at this mess, damn you, you little bitch! My French perfume—all spilled! And my precious dolls! Oh no, my darlings, what has she done to you?"

He's not surprised to find himself at Mrs. Stanley's door, which is ajar.

"Damn you, you nasty imp! So it was you, wasn't it? It was you all along—maybe in cahoots with that nigger, hmm? You white-trash devil child! Well, your partner in crime will soon be locked away—I've made sure of it. Where'd you two hide my coins, huh? I'll teach you what happens to bad girls who can't keep their dirty little hands to themselves!"

Victor hears Chrissie shriek. He pushes the door wide open and is immediately besieged by the scent of perfume. The dresser top is a mess. Some of the old woman's crystal-bottled European perfumes are lying on their bellies, their precious amber- and champagne-colored contents dripping onto the beige carpet. One of the antique dolls is on the floor, half its porcelain face devoured by a dark abyss of jagged edges. Mrs. Stanley is shaking Chrissie.

"Mommy! Granny! I want my Mommy!" the girl cries piteously.

It is Victor's turn to shout. "Mrs. Stanley, no! Stop! That is quite enough!" Victor grabs the old woman and pulls her away from the girl. The sorry sight of the child moves Victor.

Chrissie's face is red and wet. Some of the pink and white organza ruffles of her dress are hanging loose; the silk roses are torn and splayed. "There, there. Hush now, little Chrissie. Tita Vee will bring you back to Mommy and Granny." Victor wipes her tears and smoothes down her dress.

He is preparing to carry her away when he hears a groan. Mrs. Stanley lies on the floor, drawing a slow hand to her temple, half-conscious. He must have pulled the old woman so hard she lost her balance and fell.

Just then, the fire alarm rings. Victor recognizes Brenda's voice through the public address system. "Ladies and gentlemen, this is *not* a drill. I repeat. This is *not* a drill. Please don't panic, and listen carefully. A wildfire alarm has been announced for our area. We have been advised to evacuate the facility. I repeat. We need to evacuate the premises immediately. But we need to do this in an orderly manner. Please, no running, no racing to the elevators. Those who can walk by themselves, please come to the lobby now. Grab only your coats and jackets—nothing else. Those who need help getting around, don't worry. Some of our staff are already on their way to get you. Adequate transportation is on its way to bring all of you to a safe location until the threat subsides. I repeat, ladies and gentlemen . . ."

CHAPTER 17

"Please, please help me," Mrs. Stanley groans, her voice a mere whisper above the commotion outside. It sounds as if everyone is running, contrary to Brenda's advice. Victor can hear tripping and falling as well as a lot of cursing, crying, and shrieking.

Still, Victor hears Mrs. Stanley's voice above it all. "Please, boy. Please help me . . ." One of her hands reaches out to him. She grips her chest with her other hand, and her eyes plead with Victor.

It occurs to Victor that he could walk away from this. *Yes, how easy it would be!* After all, Chrissie needs to be returned to her parents and great-grandmother immediately. *There are human beings more worth saving than this bitch.* Victor remembers all the cruelties that seem natural to the woman. She reminds him so much of his mother. In fact, as Victor looks at her, he begins to see his mother's features on Mrs. Stanley's face. He shakes his head to rid himself of the frightful vision. The woman is now gasping, gripping her chest as if in extreme pain.

"Tita Vee," says a voice at the door. It's Mr. Pinkard. The old geezer's room is only a few doors away. "May I help?"

It is a time for the unexpected, it seems.

"Yes—yes, please, Mr. Pinkard. Could you bring Chrissie down to her parents and Mrs. Langley?" The girl is still hiccupping and sobbing in distress.

"Glad to. But how about Mrs. Stanley?"

"I'll take care of her."

Victor hands Chrissie over to Mr. Pinkard, who consoles the girl with, "Now, now sweetie pie. Tita Vee has to help Mrs. Stanley. Don't worry—I'll bring you to Granny, okay?"

Victor closes the door behind them and locks it. He kneels over the miserable form of Mrs. Stanley, whose face alternates with his mother's. She continues to wheeze. Her chest and neck expand and contract like the struggling gills of a fish out of water.

"My heart, it feels like my heart . . ."

How easy it would be to make this woman pay for her sins.

Mrs. Stanley manages to grab Victor's shirt. "H-help . . . help me!" Victor tries to free himself of her, but she hangs onto him with what appears to be her last wave of physical strength.

Healer, heal thyself! El Diablo, riding on the winds outside, seems to cry out to him. Victor glances at the windows, half expecting a horrific phantasm floating there. He's surprised to find that night appears to have arrived early. El Diablo's clouds of doubt have gathered over this patch of dry, burning earth. *And the sky is heavy with black sorrow—my sorrow.*

Victor screams at the invisible demon, "I am no longer a healer—it's been taken away from me! By *putas* such as this one here. Why don't you drag her back to the hell you both came from?"

Cast away this stone, hijo. Victor feels the vertigo. He shakes his head, pounding his fists on his temples, knocking off his eyeglasses. The feeling is one he hasn't experienced since he was fifteen in the cave on Mount Banahaw. His gaze is drawn to the display cabinet that contains Mrs. Stanley's antique dolls. Eyes look out at him from the previously eyeless faces—even from the broken face of the doll on the floor. He knows those eyes. They appear to be alive, not mere glass. They shine as if from the tears of the Nuestra Señora del Santo Rosario and El Negro Santo Niño de Jesus.

Victor remembers how the *santos* appeared to him last night: Mother and son, together, side by side. *The yin and yang energies that balance the force of Life itself,* the *arbolario* had taught him. *That's why up here in Mount Banahaw we call God "the Father-Mother."* He recalls also what Father John had taught him: *In God's image they were created—male and female.*

It's all coming together now. The riddle of the universe is the riddle of his life! He was created neither male nor female but as a human being who holds all of life within him so that he could bring life back to where it was cut off by the misery men and women bring upon themselves. *All are connected, after all. All is One.*

He remembers what his *Ninang* Jo-Ann wrote about his mother. *I hope, for your sake, you will be able to forgive her.*

The *arbolario's* voice rings out from the past. *A time of reckoning will come when you will have to cast this stone away or risk sinking with it. When that happens . . . you will have to save yourself—by healing yourself.*

The heat is rising in the room, but there are no flames. The medallion feels like it's branding itself onto his chest. The white burning spreads toward his heart, where it saturates him and forces him to dispense it toward his arms, his hands, until it's throbbing in his fingers, seeking release. He rips the blouse from the chest of the woman who is Mrs.

Stanley and also his mother. His fingers claw upon the bare skin until it parts to reveal flesh and bone—summoning the black heart from its nest. And what a sight it is to him, this muscle of fate and destiny carved out by sheer will. But it is barely pumping now.

Victor's hands continue their work: Massage, squeeze, release. Massage, squeeze, release. Until the cadence returns the rhythm of life to the faltering organ—and the color of death is washed away by the sanguine tide of hope.

CREDITS

Author	Victoria G. Smith
First Readers	Carrie Cantor, Diane Holmes, Deborah Bingler, James Parker, Joe Dysart, and Tracey Zabel
Copyeditors	Kelly Lauer and Ruthie Knox
Proofreader	Annamarie Bellegante
Cover Art	Hannah Irlbeck
Cover Design	Ranita Haanen
Interior Design	Williams Writing, Editing, & Design

AUTHOR'S ACKNOWLEDGMENTS

The author is grateful to the following faith healers in her life:

Her early writing critique partners—Ms. Diane Holmes, Mr. Gaylon Greer, Mr. James Parker, Ms. Deborah Bingler, Mr. Joe Dysart, and Ms. Tracey Zabel, among others, who helped shape and craft the rough drafts of her visions and turned them into realities;

Her aunts, Ms. Aida Arcilla and Mrs. Anicia Gueco, who introduced her to the worlds of literature and writing, and thus became mothers to the writer in her;

Her high school English and speech teacher, Ms. Marilyn Gueco, who inspired, expected, and exacted the best in her—and continues to do so to this day;

The Missionaries of the Sacred Heart in Angeles City, Philippines—who, through their simple, humble way of life dedicated to community service, exemplify true faith;

Her children, Francesca and Travis, whose constant expressions of pride in their mother and her work helped banish all conflicts of interest—and guilt—in a woman's aspirations for both family and career;

Her husband, Steve, who made sure she didn't starve while she got lost in her dream worlds, reminding her she still has to eat, drink, sleep, and love in the material world;

The various unnamed personalities the author has encountered in her life who have provided the inspiration and ingredients for the colorful characters in this book;

Her friends in the LGBT communities in Iowa and else-where—for their courage in confronting the demons of prejudice and intolerance that fanned the flames of a social and political revolution;

Last, but not least, the rich cultural and spiritual heritage of her native Philippines and its people, who challenge and renew her faith in human nature—always.

ABOUT THE AUTHOR

Philippine-born author and poet Victoria G. Smith's first career was in law practice. After marriage to an American that led her to immigrate to the United States, she rediscovered and pursued a childhood passion: creative writing. Her early efforts won her first place in the 2004 (Fifth Annual) Ventura County Writers Club–Ventura Country Star national short story writing contest—the first time she'd entered a writing competition. Recent distinctions include the 2015 Driftless Unsolicited Novella Award for her novella, *Faith Healer,* and semifinalist for the 2015 Elixir Press Fiction Award for her story collection, *Faith Healer and Other Stories.* Her poetry and other literary work are published by, among others, *Reed Magazine, The Greenwich Village Literary Review, The Earthbound Review, Elite Critiques Magazine, Ruminate Magazine, Westward Quarterly, The Earthen Lamp Journal, The Milo Review, Lyrical Iowa,* and *Dicta.* Her essay, "Gatekeepers and

Gatecrashers in Contemporary American Poetry: Reflections of a Filipino Immigrant Poet in the United States," appears in Black Lawrence Press's 2015 anthology, *Others Will Enter the Gates: Immigrant Poets on Poetry, Influences, and Writing in America.* Her first book of poems, *Warrior Heart, Pilgrim Soul: An Immigrant's Journey,* was published in November 2013 to critical acclaim spearheaded by *Kirkus Reviews.* Later that same year, the Chicago Filipino Asian American Hall of Fame honored her with the Outstanding Writer Award. She writes a monthly poetry column for *VIA Times Magazine.* Smith attended the 2005 UCLA Asian American–N.V.M. Gonzales Writers Program and has been featured as an emerging writer in several print media and online articles. She is currently writing her first novel, *Gabriela's Eyes,* and a second poetry collection, *Mother of Exiles.*

Updates on her literary work and author events may be found on her website, VictoriaGSmith.com.

Brain Mill Press would like to acknowledge the support of the following patrons:

Noelle Adams

Rhyll Biest

Katherine Bodsworth

Lea Franczak

Barry and Barbara Homrighaus

Kelly Lauer

Susan Lee

Sherri Marx

Aisling Murphy

Audra North

Molly O'Keefe

Virginia Parker

Cherri Porter

Erin Rathjen

Robin Drouin Tuch